Célia looked up at him then, Loukis's fierce gaze studying her intently. The steely line of his jaw tense, his hands braced as if forewarning her of some life-changing moment.

"What is it?"

"I cannot risk any further damage to my reputation. Not with my sister's happiness and future at stake. I *will* not let my mother get her hands on her, even for a minute."

She nodded, still not quite understanding where he was going with this.

"Which is why I need you to sign a nondisclosure agreement."

The statement came as a bit of a surprise to Célia, but she would have been more than happy to agree to such a thing for the happiness of the little girl who had already begun to creep into her heart.

"Is that all?" she asked, half relieved that it seemed to be the case. She took a sip of wine to steady her trembling nerves.

"No. Sadly, it is not. What I need of you now, in light of the press article, is your hand in marriage."

Pippa Roscoe lives in Norfolk near her family and makes daily promises to herself that *this* is the day she'll leave the computer to take a long walk in the countryside. She can't remember a time when she wasn't dreaming about handsome heroes and innocent heroines. Totally her mother's fault, of course—she gave Pippa her first romance to read at the age of seven! She is inconceivably happy that she gets to share those daydreams with you all. Follow her on Twitter, @pipparoscoe.

Books by Pippa Roscoe

Harlequin Presents

Conquering His Virgin Queen
Virgin Princess's Marriage Debt
Demanding His Billion-Dollar Heir

Once Upon a Temptation

Taming the Big Bad Billionaire

The Winners' Circle

A Ring to Take His Revenge
Claimed for the Greek's Child
Reclaimed by the Powerful Sheikh

Visit the Author Profile page
at Harlequin.com for more titles.

Pippa Roscoe

RUMORS BEHIND
THE GREEK'S WEDDING

Recycling programs
for this product may
not exist in your area.

ISBN-13: 978-1-335-89391-8

Rumors Behind the Greek's Wedding

Harlequin Enterprises ULC
22 Adelaide St. West, 40th Floor
Toronto, Ontario M5H 4E3, Canada
www.Harlequin.com

Printed in U.S.A.

RUMORS BEHIND
THE GREEK'S WEDDING

To Lady Penelope, a most excellent and definitely non-fictitious drinking partner. This dedication is for friends and drunken promises. *Sláinte*.

CHAPTER ONE

'*Bonsoir*, Chariton Endeavours.'

'I will speak with Célia d'Argent.'

'May I ask who's calling?'

'You can *warn* her that it's Loukis Liordis.'

'Consider her warned. What can I do for you *this time*, Mr Liordis?'

Only a brief pause hinted at any semblance of recognition from her client. And Célia d'Argent *meant* recognition. For Liordis would never lower himself to feel as human an emotion as contrition. If anything, the small moment had been one of reprimand, one that hinted it should have been for *her* to feel contrite. And normally Célia would be mortified to utter such a response. But this wasn't such an occasion. Loukis Liordis, Greek billionaire, renowned playboy and presently the biggest pain in her neck, had driven Célia beyond the brink of her usually impeccable civility.

'You answer your own phone?' he demanded as if such a thing should have been beneath her.

'I do when it is nine thirty at night, Mr Liordis.'

'What has that to do with anything?'

The absolute gall of the man!

Célia glared at her reflection in the windows of her office. Loukis might have been their first client, and might be the reason why she and her business partner Ella Riding had been able to achieve the success that they had enjoyed in the last few months, but that didn't mean she had to like him, or jump to his every command. Just the majority of them.

'You can explain to me how it is that you have spectacularly failed to deliver on your promise, Mademoiselle d'Argent.'

Célia frowned, mentally scanning through the lists of current events they had planned for him. 'I'm not quite sure what you mean, Mr Lio—'

'I will speak with Ella, then.'

Célia ground her teeth, not caring whether he heard the sound through the phone or not. She hated that his words had spread anxiety through her chest. Hated that her pulse was beginning to speed up and a wave of insecurity threatened to overwhelm her.

'I am afraid that is not possible.'

'Why not?'

'As I have explained—' *many, many times* '—Ella is presently on maternity leave.'

'Surely she is able to pick up a phone?'

'No, Mr Liordis. She is not. Now, if you could, I would like the opportunity to hear your concerns.' She wouldn't, of course. It was late, she hadn't even had dinner, and the hastily consumed half-lunch was now a distant memory.

'My concern is that you have not fulfilled your obligation.'

'Which obligation are we speaking of?'

'The one that would restore my reputation, Ms d'Argent.'

Célia dropped into the soft leather chair that was her favourite piece of office furniture and swirled round to her computer, absolutely speechless.

'You have nothing to say?'

'Forgive me, I was just checking the letterhead of our company stationery. At no point or place does it say that we are in the reputation business. Our role is—'

'I know what your role is, and don't be crass, Ms d'Argent. Ella—and by extension I presume you—knew exactly why it was that I signed on with your company. And the resulting publicity from my first event with your company was not positive.'

'I appreciate that. I do. While the charity event

backed by you and your company has given the Erythra Foundation the ability to do some incredible things in the future, personally for you, it has perhaps not gone as well as we had envisaged. Quite possibly down to the fact that you did not deem it important enough to make an appearance.'

The line went completely quiet. Icy. Frigid even. And Célia suddenly realised that she had gone too far. It was not for her to question her client. No. The headlines following the event had done that well enough. That she and they appeared aligned in the belief that he had, once again, found himself in bed with his lady *du jour*—a lady probably of statuesque physique, impeccable proportions and in all likelihood platinum blonde—was neither here nor there.

'We will talk about this further.'

Before she could even offer the possibility of a meeting, the line went dead, and the phone went limp in her hand.

What had she just done?

She *never* spoke to people that way, let alone their most valuable client. But Loukis's constant hounding over the last few months, his absolute determination for everything to be perfect had driven her and her team out of their minds. In the months since Ella had signed him in Fiji, Chariton Endeavours had taken on even more clients and had been absolutely run off their feet working hard to fulfil their promise to both the business side and the charitable side of their organisation. They'd undertaken twelve events in the last month alone, and all without Ella, who was Célia's rock, sounding board and confidante.

In truth Célia was exhausted, which was the only reason that she had let her usually ironclad guard down and said exactly what had been on her mind. She ran a slightly trembling hand over her face and finally put the phone down.

Tomorrow she would have to do damage limitation. But for now, she needed to return to her apartment and sleep. Eat. Perhaps even indulge in a cool white glass of Australian Pino Gris.

That decision rose within her like defiance, as if she still had to justify something as silly as her taste in wine to her father, even if she did imagine a look of abject horror crossing the proud Frenchman's features. His distant disapproval a constant presence in their interaction. But as Célia looked out at the Parisian streets from her window, she mentally shielded herself from being drawn down that dark path.

She grabbed her bag, her keys, locked the front door of the ground-floor office and turned onto the street only to pull up short.

The absolute gall of the man!

* * *

In a dramatic turn of his recent luck, Loukis Liordis had found a parking space just outside Chariton Endeavours about thirty minutes earlier. He had terminated his call to Célia d'Argent only ten minutes ago and was now leaning against the sleek McLaren supercar he'd leased for his time in France, scrolling through the latest headlines pontificating on his absence from the charity gala last week. Each successive screenshot fuelled an ire ignited by the steely voiced Célia.

If it hadn't been for the barely audible gasp of indignation he might not have even noticed her departure from the building. He certainly would not have *noticed* her. But that was partly due to the fact that, dressed in what could only be described as a deeply unappealing beige top, she had been camouflaged by the stonework behind her. And had it not been for a pair of black jeans he might not even have known she was there. Especially since the moment she'd caught sight of him, she had pulled up short and not moved a muscle.

He resisted the urge to roll his eyes. Barely.

'Ms d'Ar—'

'What are you doing here?' she demanded.

He'd barely taken a breath before she continued, 'You *can't* be here.' Finishing the inhalation, slowly, he locked a well-honed, utterly devastating gaze on her and tried again. 'Ms d'Argent, as I said. We need to talk further.'

'Not *now*.'

'Yes *now*. I am needed back in Greece first thing tomorrow morning,' he said, checking his watch unnecessarily, as he perfectly well knew the time, but it was not bad for an on-the-spot dramatic effect.

Having done so, he levered himself from where he leaned against the car and held open the passenger door. 'Shall we?'

'No, we shall not,' she hissed as she skirted around him and away from the open door as if he posed some great threat. Fine. He closed the door.

'Célia,' he called out before she could get much further. 'We do need to talk.'

It must have been the change in his voice that stopped her retreat. It wasn't the charming play-boy tone that had done him both great success and great damage only a few years before. Before everything he'd known had come crashing down about his ears. It wasn't the tone he'd used to seduce, or amuse, to charm, placate or cajole. Neither was it the autocratic arrogant, commanding, brook-no-argument voice he'd used on her earlier. Strangely enough it was none of the façades he'd adopted over the years, but the tone of his own true self that halted her departure.

He watched her take a deep breath and remembered just how beautiful he found her. Her face was almost startling in comparison to the bland taste in clothing. Broad features made the most of the sharp cheekbones that were contrasted with lips that were a small, delicate cupid's bow. Eyes, wide in shock, were of the purest amber. Her hair had been piled up as if thoughtlessly in a messy bun, but the little of what he could see hinted at rich auburn tones he wanted to investigate further. Her rich, creamy skin was covered in a light spattering of freckles that the horrid T-shirt did nothing for. But no matter how appealing and refreshing he found her, it was not why he was here.

'Mr Liordis. I am sorry, but I really do need to eat.'

'We have reservations at Comte Croix.'

'I… I'm hardly dressed for—'

'Anything other than paintballing? I had noticed. But as you'll be with me, I'm sure they'll make an exception.'

A blush rose to the creamiest of skin on her cheeks, blotting out the subtle shades of her freckles. He opened the door for her once again and as she passed before him he inhaled the sweet scent of orange and herbs, basil perhaps, and pressed down the urge for more. *More* was certainly *not* on the menu tonight. Or any other night, quite possibly, for the next ten years or so. In that moment he cursed his mother all over again and wished her safely and securely to hell.

Célia pressed herself deeply into the plush leather of the sleek supercar wishing she were anywhere but right there, next to Loukis Liordis. It was one thing to be sharp with him on the phone, but altogether something else to be within touching distance of such a…such a… Well, she wasn't blind. The renowned Greek billionaire playboy was utterly overwhelming in person.

From this angle she couldn't miss the thick waves of dark hair that had been pushed back from a proud forehead as if conspiring to show off his innate beauty. His brows were low above eyes that were busy scanning the lamplit Parisian streets. Eyes that she'd chastised herself already for comparing to rich espresso the one and only previous time she'd met him.

He'd come to the office before Ella's maternity leave and their brief introduction had sent seismic shock waves through Célia. Not because of any special attention he'd directed her way. No, in fact he'd barely raked a glance across her features. But that glance had fired something within her. Something she'd thought dormant. And it had been enough. Enough to warn her she would have to be on her guard around him.

Her eyes were drawn back to his tense jawline, strong enough to demand attention, despite the *keep away* aura that seemed to fill the car. The powerful angle of his cheekbones highlighted the bridge of his nose—the slight kink there hinting towards a years-old break, perhaps. But it was his lips that really got to her. They appeared ever so slightly pursed, as if intentionally drawing her gaze to the centre of his upper lip, where it swept downwards at the same point as his lower lip lent upwards just a little.

And then those lips moved. Quirking into a side-angled smile as he caught her openly staring at him.

Kill me now. Please.

She pressed even further back into the seat, trying to make herself invisible.

'If you want to move the seat back—'

'*Non, merci.*'

He simply nodded in response, never once having taken his eyes off the road, nor loosening the smile that quirked his lips.

She hated the painful blush that stole over her cheeks. Hated dealing with the rich clients Ella sourced, and wished for the hundredth time that day her best friend and business partner weren't on maternity leave. But no matter how much she did, Célia would never begrudge the happiness Ella had found with Roman. Despite a deeply rocky start, they had found their happy-ever-after. One that she couldn't ever imagine for herself. Not after...

Her thoughts were cut off as the car pulled off the road towards the large sprawling entrance of the famous Parisian restaurant. Taking a deep breath, she forced her mind into a semblance of order. 'So what did you—'

'We're here,' he announced, either purposely or unnecessarily interrupting her.

She clenched her jaw and took a deep breath in through her nose. He might be the most attractive man she'd ever seen, but he was also the most infuriating. As he exited the car, she grabbed her bag from the footwell, making sure she hadn't marked or scuffed any of the furnishings, wishing she could erase her presence from the car as much as the evening. She was about to reach for the handle when the car door swung open, to reveal Loukis standing there, offering her his hand.

Social etiquette did not compensate for rudeness, however it would be churlish to refuse, so she placed her hand in his, trying to disguise the momentary shock she felt as his fingers wrapped around hers. Tingles zipped up her hand to her wrist and forearm, raising the fine hairs as if she were in the midst of an electrical storm. A storm that held them both at the centre in a moment of complete calm. From where she sat looking up at him, he appeared to loom over her. His eyes intent, one brow slightly furrowed as if he was confused about something—a confusion she felt too as her heartbeat picked up speed to match his where she felt his pulse against her wrist.

She watched him carelessly toss the keys to a car worth more than she could dream of to the valet, and gesture for her to enter the restaurant. It was a move that even her obscenely rich father would never have made. No, there had never been anything careless about her exacting father's actions.

She felt Loukis's presence at her back as she made her way to the maître d', adopting a mask she hadn't used for years. One that implied that she was used to eating in restaurants like this for breakfast, lunch and dinner, no matter what she looked like. Even if, inside, she was experiencing an excruciating humiliation.

Over the hum in her ears she barely heard Loukis state his reservation, but she didn't miss the way the black-and-white-suited maître d' cast her a no-less-than-she-deserved disparaging look and a sudden wave of Loukis-focused resentment sliced through her. Of course she was not dressed appropriately for a restaurant of this calibre. Ten minutes ago she hadn't even known she would be here. She waited for Loukis to make some apology for her state of dress, but was surprised to find a steely glint in Loukis's eyes as if daring the man to object or find fault. Instantly his manner transformed to obsequiousness.

She followed behind the two men weaving between tables where hushed conversations, romantic assignations and even a few business deals appeared to be taking place and smiled thankfully at the now chastised man who pulled a chair out for her as if she were royal.

'May I offer you the *carte des vins*?'

'That will not be necessary. A bottle of the Pouilly-Fuissé and whatever fish main you have today.'

'Bien sûr.'

'Merci,' Célia added just before the man could beat a hasty retreat with the unseen menus. After all, she knew what it was like to be on the receiving end of Loukis's abruptness. Choosing to ignore the fact that he had not even thought to ask her wine preferences, let alone food wishes, or even possible allergies, she attempted to take at least some control back of her hijacked evening. Attempted to pull around her some of the confidence and self-assurance she felt when dealing with the charities that were her much preferred interaction.

'So, Mr Liordis, what is it that you wish to discuss?'

'I need another event.'

'Okay, did you have something in mind?'

He shook his head, his lips pulling into another moue of carelessness. 'Not particularly. Only that it must be within the next few weeks.'

Loukis watched Célia take in his directive, silently, but mind clearly racing. He had expected outrage, immediate dismissal, and certainly a great deal of objection, but no.

'It would not be realistic to expect to do so again with the Erythra Foundation.'

'Why not?' he asked, not to be petulant, but genuinely curious.

'In order to ensure that there was no oversaturation or fatigue with donations and press. Do you have another charity in mind?'

'No. But ideally it would be Greek.'

Célia nodded, pressing her hand to her rosebud lips and looking off to the side. At this angle, the length and curve of her neck were on exquisite display and he found himself almost thankful that she was wearing the horrid beige round-necked T-shirt.

The first time he'd met her, in the offices in Paris, he'd had to force himself to wrench his eyes away from her. Instantly he'd felt a pull of desire so strong and so sure that he'd been shaken by it. But even then he'd known that he couldn't entertain such a thing. Not only were they working together, but he just couldn't risk it. Not then, and certainly not now.

He was in the process of once again forcing his gaze away from that alluring curve when she turned her attention back to him.

'I would need more time than a few weeks. What is your absolute deadline?'

Loukis couldn't quite account for why her practical, no-nonsense, down-to-business approach to this conversation bothered him so much. After all, it was what he had wanted, and what he usually demanded from those he got into business with. But on Célia it seemed…unsatisfying.

'I need it done by the end of—' He cut himself off short, before revealing too much, and silently cursed the strange reaction she was provoking in him. 'By the end of June.' He had nearly said by the end of the school term. And that would have been unacceptable. It was utterly imperative that he did not reveal a single thing about why he needed this event to happen so quickly. Even the smallest detail would put everything at risk—and that he could simply not allow.

'So I have four weeks.'

'*Nai*—yes.'

'Do you have a preference over the type of event?'

'Only that it be as public and positive as possible.'

'How do you feel about art?'

'I have a few investment pieces.'

'Would you be willing to part with them?'

'If I have to.' He would be willing to part with anything if it helped his cause.

Célia's rapid round of questions was brought to a halt by the appearance of the sommelier. He proffered the bottle to him, but Loukis directed the tasting to Célia. He watched as she swirled the wine once and inhaled before tasting, then nodding her approval. Again, Loukis found himself bemused by a woman who looked as if her entire dress that evening was cheaper than the price of the bottle of wine they were about to drink. A feeling apparently shared by the sommelier, who filled their glasses modestly and left.

'What is more important to you in this event, the clientele and publicity or the funds raised for the charity?'

He knew that she would prefer the latter, but he couldn't jeopardise this. It was his last chance to bolster a ravaged reputation. Delaying the moment her displeasure would be revealed, he sidestepped the answer.

'Is this a test?'

'No, it helps determine what kind of charity to approach. If your goal is to make the greatest impact on the charity, then it would be best to approach one in great need, even if it were something that perhaps might not be on many people's radar. If, however, as I am inclined to believe, you are looking for a great *personal* impact, then a charity that could draw many celebrities, and therefore attention, would be where I start looking.'

If there was any hint of censure in her tone, Loukis could not detect it. 'No way to do both, I suppose?'

'Mr Liordis—I, *we*, match business leaders with charities. All money raised is a gift to them. And trust me, I will be charging you an obscene amount of money in order to achieve this. Money that will go towards the future investment of more money for more charities. Our endeavour may be hopeful and charitable but, make no mistake, it is also business minded.'

She was such a strange combination of steel encased in silk that he had to work hard to focus on the issue at hand and not on Célia herself.

'How obscene?'

'Very,' she said, with the smallest of smiles curving the rosebud lips upwards enticingly. She took a sip of her wine, her eyes narrowing a fraction, before putting the glass back down on the table.

'You don't like the wine?'

'I had started out the evening looking forward to an Australian Pinot Gris, a small bowl
of soup and perhaps one episode of the period
drama I'm currently watching. And yet...' She
shrugged, her hands open before her as if to say,
Here we are.

'Surely that is sacrilegious?'

'My preference in wine?'

He cocked his head to one side in answer to
her question.

'Only for purists.'

It was on his tongue to probe the question of
her purity further and realised instantly that he
would not be talking about the wine. Three years
ago nothing would have stopped the line falling
from his lips. But three years ago he had been a
very different man. At least the spell she seemed
to have woven over him had not yet quite short-
circuited his sense of decorum.

As if that self-imposed morality had returned,
he suddenly felt guilty for disrupting an evening she seemed to have very much wanted. And
for the first time that evening, he took in the
signs of exhaustion about her eyes. Very well
disguised, but still they were signs that he recognised, certainly in the first few months, if not
more, when his life had been turned upside down
by his mother three years ago. Not that he would
take them back for a second. And that timely

reminder put him back on track. Célia and her tiredness didn't matter. That she delivered what he needed did. Very much.

'So, you will arrange the event and the charity for the end of June?'

'Yes. On one condition.'

'Which is?'

'That you are present this time, Mr Liordis.'

Célia watched his eyes narrow. For a moment, it felt almost as if they had breached the business talk, as if Loukis's ruthless pursuit of a positive reputation had been forgotten. She'd felt as if he'd been about to ask something...but whatever softness, whatever sense of unmasking she had sensed had quickly withdrawn behind a look of fury.

'I do not make that request to be difficult,' she quickly added. 'If you are to achieve what you desire, then it is important that you are there.'

'I will be.'

The waiter arrived with their meals, but suddenly Célia was no longer hungry. The smell from the scallop and lobster tortellini with a bisque broth was incredible, but she couldn't shake Loukis's steady gaze. She forced herself to pick up her fork, cut into the silky pasta and the soft mousse of the filling, and as she raised it to her mouth she looked up to find his hawklike eyes still on her. As if daring her to consume it beneath his gaze.

Never had she been around a man who wielded his sensuality like an extension of himself. She couldn't deny the effect he had on her. But that didn't mean she needed to succumb to it.

The last time she had, it had proved devastating when she had realised it was not her but her father's money, her father's approval that had been her ex's end goal. She had vowed not to make the same mistake again and hadn't yet.

With that last determined cry ringing in her mind, she ate the first, second and third mouthfuls without acknowledging Loukis at all. She had focused her gaze on the plate before her and knew that the delicious meal was utterly wasted on her as her thoughts blocked the pleasure of taste.

Célia was so focused on getting to the end of the meal that, when she laid her fork down, she realised that Loukis had not only finished but was placing an alarmingly large number of euros onto the table.

'I will take you home,' he said, without sparing her a glance. Given where her thoughts had been it was hardly surprising that Célia momentarily thought he intended something else.

'That won't be necessary,' she claimed, having

absolutely no intention of letting Loukis Liordis anywhere near her apartment.

He pierced her with a look that she was sure would have wilted many a woman throughout the years. 'That is not how I was raised.'

'And that has nothing to do with me. I can find my own way home, but thank you for the offer.'

He followed so close behind her as they wound their way out of the restaurant that Célia was sure that she could feel the heat of his body pressing against her, speeding her departure from Comte Croix.

He waited until she had arranged for the valet to call her a cab, spinning his keys around his forefinger not with impatience, but habit, she supposed. When the car arrived, he opened the door for her, and left it open as she settled into the sleek town car.

'I look forward to hearing from you as the plans develop for the event. In the meantime, Ms d'Argent, do yourself and the world a favour and burn that T-shirt.'

He closed the door before she could even respond and disappeared into the night.

The absolute gall of the man!

CHAPTER TWO

TWENTY-FIVE DAYS, FOUR hundred and thirty-three emails, one hundred and twenty-eight hours of meetings, one hundred and nineteen invitations, and two flights later, Célia found herself in a stunning white-walled exhibition space overlooking the Acropolis in Athens.

If she had been tired the evening she had gone for dinner with Loukis, she was exhausted tonight. But in just a few hours, the event Liordis had demanded, negotiated, tweaked, argued and begrudgingly agreed to, would be over. And she could sleep. Finally. Perhaps even have *one* day where she didn't have to have a single tense conversation with the Greek billionaire.

Still, she could argue that what they had managed to achieve together in such an impossibly brief time was nothing short of miraculous. She might have managed to sound confident back in the Comte Croix in Paris, but the panic that had beset her once the anger from his comment about her clothing had receded along with the image of him standing there watching the car turn the corner had been swift and intense. And certainly enough to distract her from the devastating effect he'd had on her in person.

She passed between the two large stone columns that would greet their guests and onwards into the open white-walled space, contrasting against the dark granite flooring and rough concrete ceiling that lined the repurposed warehouse. It was a fairly new gallery, but absolutely perfect for the event.

The clean tones offset the collection of admittedly impressive pieces Loukis had managed to get his hands on, either from his own collection or donated from equally wealthy contributors. Bright colours screamed from the canvases of some of the world's most famous modern artists. Muted tones soothed from older masterpieces, and shadows were cast from inconceivable sculptures from throughout the last century.

For a moment, Célia was lost in the sheer beauty of what surrounded her until the click of high heels made their way towards her. She turned to find Sia Keating, the art valuer from the privately owned international auction house Bonnaire. As always, Célia found herself unable to look away from the glorious titian hair that haloed her face and neck.

'Célia, I'm so pleased I got to see you before I left,' Sia said as she took Célia into a warm embrace.

'Me too,' she replied. 'I can't thank you enough for doing this at such short notice.'

'It's my pleasure, and for a very good cause. Is everything in place?'

'Yes, each piece's documentation is present and correct and, if I may say so, *very* impressive.'

Célia smiled. That final check meant that the event could go ahead as planned. 'And having Bonnaire as backers for it is a real coup.'

Sia's smile dimmed a little. 'Well, they were happy to do so, provided I took the valuation on my own time.'

Célia frowned. 'On your own time?'

'I had lots of holiday to use anyway. And it's *almost* on the way to the Emirates.'

'I'm sure we could—'

'No,' Sia said with a genuine smile this time. 'Really, it's fine. It's nice to be part of something like this. And frankly I was lucky enough to get a job with them anyway.'

Célia placed a comforting hand on Sia's. They had become fast friends since first meeting at a charity gala event a few years ago and bonded over the difficulties with their parents.

'Dare I ask?' Sia questioned.

'I haven't seen either of them in five years,'

Célia replied, knowing that Sia was asking after her parents.

An alarm beeped on Sia's phone and she looked apologetic as she reached into her handbag to retrieve it. Shaking her head again, 'I'm so sorry. The flight is due to leave in just a few hours.'

Wishing Célia the best of luck for the evening, Sia departed with promises to meet up soon in Paris.

Once again Célia was alone in the grand space. Only this time echoes of an old hurt were her companion. She flicked out her fingers from her hands as if she could expel the painful sensation gathering within her body as she walked amongst the pieces of art that would hopefully net the charity a large sum of money and, of course, garner a great deal of positive press for Loukis.

Three rooms over, towards the back of the gallery, there were forty-five staff hired for the evening preparing canapés and drinks for the attendees. The master of ceremonies for the evening had arrived and was getting himself ready. But just for a moment, Célia had the space to herself and she drew in a deep breath to calm the nerves roiling in her stomach.

Rarely had she been at the front and centre of events like this. Ella usually gloried in this role. Ella, who had been worried when Célia had called to update her on the event. She hadn't missed the brief pause that spoke of her concerns. She hadn't missed the carefully constructed sentences gently probing if she might be taking on too much, or whether she might actually not be able to pull it off.

All of which had only driven Célia further. She now had as much invested in the event as Loukis. A brief flare of irritation welled in her chest as her thoughts turned to him, especially as since she had last seen him, far too much of her time had suddenly seemed preoccupied with her own clothing.

She pulled a slight grimace as she looked down at her black trousers and white silky top. It was definitely better than the beige T-shirt but she was sure that Loukis would manage to find fault with it. A part of her had wanted to find something that would wipe the disdain from his face the next time they met, but she had neither the time nor the money to do so.

Every bit she earned went into either the company or her home. Living in Paris, alone now—without Ella to share the rent—she'd had to move into a new apartment and, although she loved it dearly, it was still a drain on her earnings. Ella and Roman had offered to buy somewhere in Paris but Célia couldn't, wouldn't, take that. It wasn't so much a case of cutting her nose off out of spite, more an awareness of how much she valued her own independence after all those years. Her father would be horrified to see the small loft apartment she had squeezed herself into. It was a far cry from the palatial estate she had grown up in as a child, before being sent to boarding school. And while it had been the height of luxury and status, she shivered at the memory of the way silence had echoed amongst the rooms. Seen and not heard, had been her father's idiom. And for the millionth time, she wondered if it would have been different had she been born the son that her father had so desperately wanted. The heir to the business that was her father's sole focus. Would that have prevented the endless well of disapproval she had felt from her father—even as she tried to emulate his path by going into computer sciences and engineering?

When she heard the determined clipped tones of shoes on the sleek flooring, she turned, wondering if Sia had forgotten something, and stopped short.

Loukis stalked towards her, his gait somehow both lazy and predatory, careless yet alluringly so. Dressed in a black tux, his white shirt undone at the collar, the tie balled in his fist, he looked as if he were just finishing his evening rather than starting it. As if he had just departed some mysterious woman's bed. The thought sent images crashing through her brain and short-circuited the carefully prepared welcome she had wanted to greet him with.

'Is everything ready?' he demanded across the space as if he already had somewhere else to be, someone else on his mind.

She took in a breath she hoped would calm the frustration that seemed to be a constant companion to his sudden appearances.

'Yes.'

'*Kalós,*' he said, scanning the space quickly with an assessing gaze before he reached her.

'Are *you* ready?' she queried, cursing her words the moment his eyes returned to hers and pinned her with an angry stare.

'*Nai.*'

'Really?' she asked again, despite his assurance. Somehow in all their conversations she'd become strangely touched by his use of half-Greek, half-English words, their meaning evident by the context. It was not the suave language of the playboy, but a signal of understanding, of trust in her and her abilities.

She held her hand out for the tie still clenched in a vicelike grip, wondering which Loukis she would get this evening. She had seen his determined side, she had seen the charming side as he had flirted over the phone with her usually sternly efficient assistant, the result of which was for her to descend into a useless heap of blushes and giggles. Only once had she seen what she thought might be the true Loukis. When he had said that they needed to talk in a tone that had stopped her hasty departure, before they had gone to Comte Croix.

Frowning, he held out the crumpled tie, which she smoothed before stepping closer to him and looping it up over his head. The move had begun as an automatic thing. The mirror image of a memory she had from her childhood. Of watching her mother doing this for her father before every dinner event they attended. Even as her hands crossed over the silky black material, looping it into a bow tie, Célia wondered what on earth she was doing, aching from the past and yearning for something she should not want from the present.

The scent from his aftershave, spicy and earthy, drifted towards her as if propelled by the heat from his body, crashing against her in waves. Refusing to look up at him, unable to face what must have been confusion at her actions, she concentrated on knotting the silks in the right way and just about resisted placing her hands on his chest once she had done. They fell uselessly beside her once she had pulled the silk tight and stepped back, looking out to what must have been a Hockney to disguise her own embarrassment.

'I don't think that anyone has ever done that for me before.'

Loukis watched her shrug a shoulder as if to say it was nothing, but the small gesture had exposed the sleek line of her neck and collarbone and obliterated any sense of casualness the moment might have conveyed. The moment she had looped the tie over his neck, she had brought them so close he could smell her shampoo, orange blossom and citrus. He'd had to look away, jaw clenched and body steeled against the sudden shocking wave of arousal she had ignited. If he'd been tense when he had arrived, he was now rigid.

But any thoughts of sensual delight provoked by Célia were doused with the reminder of why he had been so stressed upon his arrival. Sobbing ten-year-olds had that effect. Sobbing ten-year-old sisters tended to drive him beyond despair.

'Why do I have to go...? Why are you making me do this...? Please, Loukis, I don't want to go with her...'

The ache in his chest mixed with fury and an impotence, a helplessness, that Loukis simply refused to accept.

'The MC is here?'

Célia stepped away, as if sensing the swift change in mood from whatever had just passed between them.

'Yes.'

'And the—'

'Valuation has been done, the staff are preparing the food and drink for this evening. The red carpet is lined with a roaring crowd of paparazzi—in case you came in the back way—and all but three invitations have been accepted. We should have a full turnout.'

Loukis nodded, heedless of the way she had interrupted him.

'Good. We should go.'

'Go?' Célia asked. 'What? Why would we—'

'We need to make an appearance on the red carpet. My limousine is waiting at the back to circle around the block so we can make our grand entrance.'

The horror covering Célia's features would have been funny had it not been such a shocking waste of time.

'No. I'm not… I cannot—'

'You can and you will.'

She was shaking her head now and backing away from him as if he posed some great physical threat.

'I did not agree to that and…no. No, Loukis, I will not be walking the red carpet with you. I will not get drawn into whatever publicity you are courting. I can't be—'

'Associated with me?' Loukis demanded. As if he didn't have enough reasons to regret his wayward youth. A wave of exasperation rode over him, his usual defences having been brought down by Annabelle's recent misery. At one time in his life, he'd had nothing more to think of than his own sensual pleasures. With hindsight he could see the desperate need to escape, to lose himself in whatever delighted him after years of a bitter, emotionally neglected childhood. To protect himself, even, from all the hurt that it had brought.

He had immersed himself in whatever and whoever he could find, courting scandalous headlines even as he sought, almost childishly, to illustrate just how little he cared. How he had laughed as each of the world's news stations and papers had reported his latest exploit in competition with his even more scandalous mother.

But he did care. Cared that Célia seemed so horrified by being seen with the legendary playboy. It hurt, more, because in the last month they had worked so closely together on tonight's event, he'd inch by inch shown a little of his true self. He'd relaxed into her strangely satisfying blunt honesty and thought that just maybe she'd seen him as more than a headline. But he should have known better.

'No, Loukis, it's not what you—'

'It's fine,' he said, cutting off any further words with a hand slashed through the air. Without casting another glance her way, he spun on his heel and exited the room, pulling slightly at the bow tie's hold around his neck.

It was time to refocus on why this night was so important. Three years ago, his mother had unceremoniously dumped a seven-year-old girl on his doorstep, without any other explanation than 'sister', and departed. No return date, no apology, no financial assistance and no belongings—clothes even. Nothing. Until six months ago, legal documents bearing the word 'custody' plunged a knife into his heart.

By the time he'd walked through the kitchens and passed staff too preoccupied with their tasks to give him a second look, he'd managed to calm his breathing. By the time he slid into the back of the sleek limousine he'd decided it was better she was not by his side and was already cursing whatever accidental instinct had prompted such a demand. And by the time the town car had circled the building to draw up at the top of the red carpet, to a hail of flashbulbs, he had a particularly charming smile in place.

He opened the door to the limo himself, not

waiting for the driver, and stepped out onto the carpet. Initially he'd been against the idea, but had been won over by the calibre of celebrities Célia had somehow managed to draw to the event. He was not so vain as to think for a second that it was because of him. Yes, his name held not inconsiderable weight in the business world, and his private fortune had amassed into the billions, courtesy of his father's years of hard work. But savvy, intellect and, as he'd once heard an Englishman say, gift of the gab had nearly trebled the shipping company's income.

All of which had made his board members very happy and his mother even more avaricious. Especially in the years since his father's death. But it was the years before his father's death that had created the most damage. Watching his father slowly lose a piece of himself each time his mother disappeared with yet another lover before he finally broke had taken its toll on Loukis, and ensured that the one surefire way of getting what he wanted—sole custody over his sister—was completely untenable. Nothing would persuade him to enter into the devil's bargain of unholy matrimony, not even to appease the court's outdated impression of what 'family' should look like. After all, that mirage of a family unit had done him no favours.

So no. The only conceivable way forward, the

only way to change the tide of public opinion on a reputation he hadn't actually lived up to in the last three years, was this. This event. It had to be absolutely perfect. So as the flashbulbs strobed through the night, he smiled his most charming smile, waved and stopped to speak with reporters even though his skin crawled and his face hurt. Perhaps Célia had been right not to accompany him along the carpet after all.

'It's been such a wonderful event, Célia. You've done really incredible things here, not to mention the life-changing amount of money raised.'

'You're very welcome. Estía is a wonderful charity and it's one very close to Loukis's heart.'

The wryly raised eyebrow from Estía's CEO was hardly subtle, but he accepted her statement without comment.

'Loukis Liordis has been deeply involved with every decision on this evening's event. It was incredibly important to him that it was perfect.' Nothing Célia had said was a lie—it was, however, open to interpretation. And looking at the now thoughtful expression on Mr Sideris' features, she felt at least satisfied that she had worked hard to achieve both aims of the night. To help the charity *and* Loukis's reputation.

Throughout the evening she had caught glimpses of him as he met and spoke with everyone present, celebrity and charity member alike. She'd tried to ignore the way that every adoring female gaze followed him—not that she could blame them. He was simply stunning—magnetic even as each woman present seemed to be drawn towards him consciously or otherwise. Célia had tried to block out how tactile he was, always touching someone on the arm, leaning forward into space Célia considered far more personal than not. But what she really marvelled at was how unconscious it seemed to be for him. He just…*did* that. For a person who shrank back into the shadows at every opportunity, Célia found herself oddly jealous at the ease with which he interacted with others.

'That's very kind of you to say, Mr Sideris.'

Célia jumped at the sudden and shocking proximity of the man she had just been thinking of. An action painfully visible to both men. She felt the blush rising on her cheeks and cursed her pale skin tones. Loukis speared her with an odd expression—one of either confusion, disdain, or even quite possibly both—before turning back to Estía's CEO.

'I very much look forward to doing business with you again,' he said, grasping Sideris' hand in his own.

'Likewise, Mr Liordis. Likewise,' returned the

CEO, before departing with the wife that had been waiting patiently in the background.

Célia retrieved her phone from her trouser pocket, most definitely a benefit of her attire that evening, and clicked through the security pin code to retrieve the web browser she had found earlier.

'One roaring success, Mr Liordis.'

He took the phone from her hand, using the tips of his fingers as if not wanting to make physical contact with her. It made her plunge her hand into her pocket. It made her feel…hurt having seen him be so open with all the other guests present that evening.

'What am I looking at?'

'The online results for this evening's events,' she said, the excitement at their achievement that evening cutting through any preceding thoughts. 'With over two hundred and fifty thousand unique visitors to Estía's website in the last four hours—'

'Two hundred and fifty thousand? That doesn't seem that much.'

'Loukis, you're incredible. Truly. But you're not a Kardashian. It's great, trust me.'

'For who, Estía or me?'

'For *both*,' she replied, feeling like growling. 'If it helps at all, then the majority of those visitors' page impressions were to your bio on the site. But perhaps you'll be happier with the fact that you're currently across nearly every social media site, four international news agency websites and you'll be on the front cover of the early morning edition of *The Times*. In five different countries.'

'What about the American press?'

She was going to kill him. She was *really* going to kill him. His inquisition seemed solely focused on his own ego and it was destroying any sense of pride and accomplishment she felt at having not only pulled the whole event off— *in little less than a month*—but also ensuring it was actually a success, despite what Liordis apparently thought. She snatched her phone from his hands, unable to avoid that irritating zing that served only to fuel her ire, and walked away.

'Is it going to be in the American press?' he called after her.

'Why does it matter?' she tossed over her shoulder.

'It just does, Célia.'

He was using that tone again. The one that she instinctively knew was more *him* than anything else he'd said. It caused her to pull up short. Again. She didn't need to check her phone for the answer. 'Yes,' she said, finally turning back to him. 'Happy now?'

'Nai.'

He didn't look happy. He looked more deter-mined and more than a little...triumphant? It was an odd expression. It was...utterly devastating. Her heart began to pound in her chest and she wanted to run. To get away from him as fast as possible.

'Where are you going?' he demanded.

'Back to my hotel. I have an early morning flight back to Paris.'

'I'll take you.'

'I can find my own—'

'I'll take you, Célia.'

She shivered, hating the effect of his words on her already overly sensitised thoughts. For a moment, the promise hung on the air between them—as if he, too, realised the double enten-dre. Purposefully sidestepping that thought, she wondered how she *would* get back to her hotel. Exhausted and not speaking Greek, she decided Loukis's offer was the easiest and quickest solution.

'Fine.'

'Then you are going the wrong way. My car is waiting in a side street. Best to avoid any fur-ther press.'

He held out an arm to guide her and although he didn't touch her, didn't place it against the white silk of her top, as she passed him she felt the heat of his palm as if he had rested his hand against the lower part of her back.

They made their way through nearly deserted kitchens and out into the alley where, as promised, Loukis's limousine was waiting for them. The driver leaning against the car hastily jumped to attention, but not quickly enough for Loukis, who opened the door and ushered her inside.

The warm, dark interior was a complete contrast to the shocking white walls and brightly coloured paintings that had decorated Célia's last six hours and she closed her eyes, taking the first nearly calm breath that evening, desperately seeking that sense of excitement and pleasure at a job well done. Anything other than the awareness of the man sliding in beside her.

'Champagne?'

'Non, merci,' she replied.

She hadn't touched a drop of the bubbly alcohol in years, because the nutty dry taste on her tongue embodied far too much the hurts of the past. To Célia it reminded her of disapproval, of superiority, of desperately waiting for the moment that her father would finally see her. Would finally recognise her. Love her.

She rubbed at the headache forming at her temples. Too much of that evening, too much of Loukis, seemed to remind her of that. Of powerful men who only wanted one thing…one thing that had never been *her*.

And she hated that sense of desperation yawning within her. Because of what it had driven her to; the times she had tried, and tried, to be what her father wanted, to choose a profession, a career that would somehow bring her closer to him. Choices that had led her to develop designs that had unwittingly caused such devastation.

And for the first time, she wondered how many charities she would need to help in order to pay off the taint on her soul. To compensate the damage done by her naïve technical designs. Ones she had hoped would help, but instead had been used for destruction. By her father. The man whose name she no longer bore. The man she had not seen in five years.

'Are you—'

Whatever Loukis had been about to say, as the limousine pulled out into the busy night-time traffic, was cut off by the ringing of his mobile phone.

'Nai?'

Before he could press on, Célia felt the temperature in the back of the town car drop to below freezing. A stream of urgent Greek poured into the space, causing her to shift and shiver in concern. Something was wrong. Terribly wrong.

Loukis leant forward, pounding on the screen to the driver, and seemed to be directing words both to him and down the phone.

Célia wrapped her arms around her waist, sensing that it would be impossible for her to interrupt and ask what was going on. As Loukis continued to bark words into the phone, his free hand went to his hair, shoving it back from his face in desperation. He looked as if he wanted to tear it from his head.

The limo pulled around in a shocking U-turn, sending her sprawling against him, her hand landing against his thigh and her chest pressing against the stiff outline of his shoulder. He reached to settle her, his hand against her forearm, holding her until the car had righted itself, and finally hung up the phone, staring ahead of him as if he had just seen a ghost.

Célia bit down on her lip, stopping the questions running through her mind.

'We have to… I…'

She had never seen Loukis stuck for words and could not even begin to imagine what had happened to cause him such…panic.

'We don't have time—'

'It's okay,' she assured him.

'I—'

'Loukis, it's okay,' she repeated, pulling herself from his grasp, knowing that they were no longer going to her hotel room, and very much hoping that what she had said to him was the truth.

CHAPTER THREE

LOUKIS LAUNCHED HIMSELF from the car before it could even draw to a halt. His blood was pounding so loudly in his ears that he barely heard Célia follow him from the car and up the steps of his Athens estate. The door swung open before he could grab the handle and the terrified face of the usually competent American nanny loomed in the doorway.

'Have you found her?' he demanded.

Her tear-stained cheeks trembled as she shook her head in denial. Tara had been with them for the three years since Meredith had deposited his sister on his doorstep, a seven-year-old who had spoken not even a word of Greek and had since found the language deeply difficult to master.

He bit out a curse and ran his fingers through already tousled hair. He stalked to the bottom of the staircase in the hallway and shouted, 'Annabelle,' as loudly as he could. Hoping that if she were somewhere in the house, the sheer ferocit of his tone would draw her out. That she would sense his fear and come running. But only silence met his call.

He spun round on the poor upset woman just as Célia reached the entrance to the estate, staring confusedly between him and Tara. He didn't have time for this, didn't have time—or words—to explain to Célia what he'd brought her into.

'What happened?' he demanded.

'I don't know…she had been upset all afternoon. She didn't want to go…' At this, Tara cast a look towards Célia, clearly unsure about what she could and couldn't say in front of this stranger. Loukis waved a hand—he'd deal with that later. Now, he just needed to find Annabelle. Tara took a deep breath. 'She doesn't want to go to her mother. I'd put her to bed at seven this evening, just like always, and when I went to check on her, she….' Tara's eyes welled and a half-wail threatened to undo him.

She could be anywhere. Panic, like he'd never known before, reached into his chest and pulled at his breath. His hands began to tremble as if he no longer had control over his own body.

'How old is she?' Célia asked, continuing in English, clearly grasping the situation from the brief conversation.

'Ten,' replied Tara.

'And did you go somewhere this afternoon, or are there any favourite hiding places she had?'

Loukis's mind flashed back to his own childhood. His own favourite hiding places and the many, many times that he'd run away himself. *Christos*, Meredith had been back in her daughter's life for only six months and the effect on Annabelle was already devastating. She had never run away before. She had never run from *him*.

He eyed a vase on the table stand in the hallway and wanted to throw it against the wall, anything to expel some of this fear, this anger, this rage.

'Did you check the pool house? I'm going to check the pool house.'

'Should we call the police?'

Tara's question stopped him in his tracks. Should he? He hated the fact that the first place his mind went was not the immediate safety of his sister, but the long term. If he called the police, it would be on record, and it would desperately affect the custody battle—no matter that Meredith would have been the main cause of it. But if something had happened to Annabelle…

'Do you think that she could have left the estate?' Célia questioned. 'Would she have been able to leave through the front door—or anywhere from the garden?'

Tara shook her head. 'I've been in the sitting room, so would have known if she'd passed me to get out through the front door. And the garden is walled and gated...' but she shrugged her shoulders helplessly.

Célia rubbed Tara's arm a little—a gesture of consolation and support for a complete stranger that struck him deeply for just a second, before all the fears and thoughts crashed through his painfully chaotic brain.

'Then we give it an hour, I think, before calling the police. But perhaps you could ask the driver to check the surrounding streets, or any parks she liked to visit?'

Tara cast a hopeful look towards Loukis, who nodded his assent. The nanny disappeared out into the night while thoughts of Annabelle being alone out there in the dark shook him to the core.

'Why don't you go and check the pool house, as you said, and perhaps any other places in the garden. In the meantime, I'll head to the top of the house and work my way down. Perhaps fresh eyes might help.'

He was as thankful for her calm efficiency as he was irritated by it. He was usually the calm head in the crisis, *he* usually knew what to do. But this?

'If I find her...'

'She speaks English fluently,' he said, before heading out into the night himself, his only thought to find Annabelle.

As Célia made her way up the large sweeping marble staircase, she struggled for some of the calm she had somehow been able to project on two people who seemed absolutely terrified beyond their wits. Had she made the right suggestion not to call the police? Was it actually the height of stupidity not to do so?

But that was only one path her mind took. The other was that Loukis had a ten-year-old child. He must have been quite young when she was born, not that that mattered. But the fact that he had apparently been living a playboy lifestyle while his child had been in nappies? Was it possible he had not known about her then? Indignation about his playboy lifestyle all the while he had a child reared in her mind. Could he have done that knowing he had a daughter? Her mind was spinning with all the unanswered questions.

As a child Célia had never run away. It had simply never occurred to her to disappoint her father even more than he already had been. She had grown up with impossible wealth, but the cost of it had been loneliness and emotional distance. Célia's birth was traumatic for her mother, who had then been unable to carry another child, thus failing to provide her father with the heir he had so desperately wanted. And so he had simply removed himself from her life, long before she could do and had done the same. She would spend hours trying vainly to catch even a glimpse of him when he finally returned from his office, or the few days he might be home at the same time as her boarding school holidays. All that hope, all that yearning still ran through the pain and anger she'd drawn around her in the last five years.

But she forced those aside as she came to the top of the large estate, sighing at the sheer number of rooms and spaces that a ten-year-old could hide in and not even knowing where to begin.

She walked along the hallway all the way to the end and opened the door to a master bedroom. Instantly she was hit by a familiar scent— Loukis's aftershave. Lit only by the moon, the room was cast in shadow, but she could make out an impossibly large bed with dark sheets, perfectly made. Everything about the room was neat and tidy, and Célia struggled with the feeling of imposing, of trespassing where she should not. But she did have a missing girl to find, so she quickly and efficiently looked wherever she thought this Annabelle might be able to hide. Beneath the bed, the deeply impressive walk-in wardrobes, the en suite bathroom. All the while unable to shake the sense of *him* around her.

Having thoroughly investigated the space, she left, quietly closing the door as if somehow that could excuse the intrusion she felt she had made.

The next room down on the left was…completely different. The lights had been left on, so the beautiful soft pink walls seemed to glow. White, fluffy fairy lights hung against the wall beside another impossibly large bed with a princess canopy. Célia couldn't help but smile, thinking it close to every little girl's dream. Unlike the near ruthless tidiness of Loukis's room, Annabelle's was strewn with open books, stickers, pens and cut pieces of paper. Clothes were scattered on the floor, stuffed toys in various heaps marked the edges of the room, shoes and a dressing gown discarded lazily by the wardrobe.

Célia frowned. Surely if Annabelle had run away from the house, she would have taken her shoes and even the coat that still hung on the back of the door. Not knowing what could have set the girl off, aside from Tara saying that she hadn't wanted to go and see her mother, it was hard to say just how far she might have wanted to run. But Célia didn't think that she really would have gone far.

As she made her way out into the hall, she thought she heard something. A sniffle, perhaps? But not from the room she had just left. She glanced up and down the hallway, seeing several doorways that could lead off into more rooms. She was about to leave when she heard the sound again.

Torn between not wanting to scare the girl and letting Loukis know that she might have found the child, she realised that even Loukis would want Annabelle to be the priority. Célia popped back into the girl's room and retrieved the stuffed toy that took pride of place on Annabelle's bed and returned to the hallway, folding herself into a cross-legged position on the floor.

'Well, Mr Bear. It's very nice to meet you. But I wondered if you could help me, because I'm looking for a little girl called Annabelle. You see, Loukis is very worried about her...'

She held the toy to her ear, hoping that this would work. Otherwise, she really was going to look quite foolish.

'I know,' she said replying to nothing. 'It's very hard for an adult to be so scared.'

A crack appeared in a doorway a few metres from where Célia was sitting. It was just a sliver of darkness, but it was enough to give Célia hope.

'I'm sure it's hard for a bear to be scared too,' she pressed on, asking whoever it was out there to forgive her for laying such a guilt trip on a ten-year-old child.

The door widened a bit more and Célia was

sure that she could make out a little foot at the bottom. Perhaps even a flash of pink pyjamas.

'But I am sure that Annabelle is okay, Mr Bear.'

'His name is Alfred,' came a voice from behind the door.

'Alfred,' Célia exclaimed. 'What a truly marvellous name. It is very nice to meet you Alfred. My name is Célia.' She shook the little bear's paw all the while studiously ignoring Annabelle and instead focusing on the bear as if he were the most important thing in the world. Célia's heartbeat had risen dramatically the moment she sensed Annabelle, but now she knew she was safe in the house, her pulse slowed even as she was desperate to call out to Loukis.

'Is Loukis very scared?'

'A little,' she said, finally turning to take in the girl. 'But nothing he won't get over,' she said with a smile at the little dark, curly-haired girl with tears shimmering in her eyes.

'I didn't want him to be scared.'

'I know, *ma chérie.*'

Annabelle came to sit beside her on the floor of the hallway. 'Why am I a cherry?'

Célia smiled, a true, wide glorious smile. 'Well, you are deliciously pink, and sweet and I think...yes, I can most definitely see a stalk growing from the top of your head.'

'No, you *can't*.' Annabelle giggled.

'Yes, I *can*,' Célia insisted, grasping nothing but air just a few inches above the girl's head. 'See?'

She couldn't help but laugh as Annabelle craned her neck to try and look above her head and was delighted when Annabelle joined in.

Through the bannisters, just over Annabelle's shoulder, she caught sight of Loukis, who immediately pressed a finger to his lips, clearly not wanting to interrupt. She saw him lean back against the wall, and inhale a silent, but shaky breath of relief.

And as the adrenaline crashed down through her body, Célia was torn between an irascible fury that he was foisting this sweet adorable little girl on a mother who she clearly did not want to see, presumably so he could go about his playboy ways, and the swipe of her conscience reminding her that it was none of her business either way.

'I think that Alfred is a little tired after all this evening's excitement. What about you?' she said to Annabelle.

Loukis closed the door to Annabelle's bedroom, putting the phone he'd just checked back into his pocket and heaving the deepest sigh of relief that he had ever breathed. The moment he had heard Annabelle's giggle from the floor above, he'd wanted to sweep her up in his arms and never let go. And it was precisely that which made him surer than ever that he could not let Meredith gain custody. Not even for a second. Annabelle had been so devastated by the return of her absent mother she had run away. She could have been…

He stopped his mind from reaching all the dark places that had nearly consumed him in the last two hours. She was safe. And he would do *whatever* it took to keep her that way. Especially in light of the press's recent and most devastating blow. He stalked down the stairs and into the living area where Célia was sitting having a drink with Tara, who was still looking deeply upset.

'Mr Liordis, I'm so very—'

He cut off her words with a slash of his hand through the air. 'It's fine. She's safe. You may go,' he instructed. He certainly didn't need a witness to his next conversation with Célia.

Tara put down her drink, casting a watery-eyed glance at each of them, before retreating upstairs to her room.

As Célia moved to do the same with her glass, he took a seat opposite her, leaning forward and resting his elbows on his knees. She seemed to realise that the gesture spoke of a future conversation and pulled the glass back to her as if unsure of what was going to happen next.

'I…' He stalled, trying to order his thoughts. Knowing what needed to be done and yet somehow wanting to put it off, if only for a moment. 'Thank you. For this evening.'

Célia nodded, but said nothing. He could sense a storm brewing behind that burnt amber gaze. It vibrated from her, lashing against his skin from across the space between them. Her cupid's bow lips had thinned, emotion had painted rose-coloured slashes on her cheekbones, and he welcomed it. Welcomed the fight he desired as much as she seemed to. Anything to release all this pent-up, unspent adrenaline.

'Out with it,' he commanded.

'It has absolutely nothing to do with me, Mr Liordis.'

He gave her a look that communicated the exact thought of, *Oh, come on*.

'Fine. Really? You leave a deeply distraught ten-year-old girl with a nanny who, by all accounts, was on the phone to her boyfriend for half the bloody night, while you were out there schmoozing with celebrities for what? Restoring your all-important reputation?'

'If you'll remember, one of your conditions about holding the event in the first place *dictated* my presence.'

'Not to the detriment of the peace of mind of a *child*.'

'Yet when I *did* do precisely as you ask on the night of the Kinley charity event, I was lambasted by both the press *and* you,' he ground out, barely able to keep the frustration from his tone.

Brows furrowed, Célia seemed to take in this new piece of information.

'Why not just say it was because of your daughter?'

'She's not my daughter.' He'd known that would have been her conclusion. It would have been anyone's conclusion. Especially for someone with his reputation. 'She is my sister.' He took a deep breath, knowing that he had no other choice but to come clean with the entire story—something he hadn't done with his closest friends, let alone a stranger. Though he couldn't really say that Célia felt like a stranger as such. But if he was to get her to agree to his plan, he would have to explain.

'My half-sister,' he clarified. 'Meredith, our mother,' he said, barely able to say the words without scorching disdain dripping from every syllable, 'had her five years after my parents had divorced.'

'Who is…?' Célia trailed off, appearing to regret her interruption.

'The father?' He shrugged. 'If Meredith knows, she's never said. I would imagine that he's not an option, otherwise Annabelle would never have ended up with me. Three years ago she was dropped off on my doorstep, with no belongings, clothing, books, toys or otherwise and I was told by Meredith, as she practically leapt into the waiting car, to "take care of her".'

'Annabelle has not seen Meredith or heard from her since that day. Until six months ago. Her lawyers got in touch with mine to demand her return. As if she was a package to be sent back to its sender.'

Loukis leaned forward into the space between them, placing his elbows on his knees. 'For three years, Annabelle has lived with me. I have seen to her every need from schooling, to holidays, to play dates, and music lessons. She barely remembers Meredith, aside from the ache of abandonment, and I have no intention of letting my sister be taken away to another country by a mother who all but eschews any semblance of maternal instinct.'

Célia seemed to consume the information readily enough, even though he knew that she could barely conceive of the part that she would, now, have to play in his obscene family drama.

'That is why you've been working to redeem your reputation.' It was a statement rather than a question, but he nodded anyway.

'But why keep everything such a secret?' she queried.

'Because I know what Meredith is like. I know how she twists and turns things, how her scheming little mind works,' he concluded, thrust back into the sealed records of his parents' divorce. How she had turned everything around to make every act, every word a mirror of what it had been in truth. 'And because I know, with everything in me, that this is just about money. She doesn't care about Annabelle one bit,' he said, concluding silently that the reason he knew this was because she had never cared about *him*. Meredith had eventually shown her true colours, and he half hoped that she would do so again, if it wouldn't inflict further pain on his sister.

'Then why are you telling me?' Célia asked, her amber gaze once again warily watchful.

'I need you to take a look at something for me.' He offered her his phone, open to the search engine tab that displayed the shocking headline *Liordis At It Again With Mystery Woman!*

The three grainy photos showed Loukis ushering Célia into the limousine, the car doing its sudden, urgent U-turn, and the two of them rushing into the house. The speculation about the urgency of their desire for each other was bald and blatant.

The shock that crossed Célia's features as she read, the way her hand went to her lips as if to stifle some inaudible gasp soothed a little of the anger coursing through his veins. Little, but not enough. Everything he had done in the past three years, all of the attempts to redeem his impossibly tarnished reputation, had burned to dust.

Célia took in the headlines and the black and white photos of herself and Loukis. She hated that some unseen person had followed them, had taken pictures of such a vulnerable moment for Loukis. When she was a child, her father had gone to great lengths to keep her and her mother away from the prying eyes of the press. But attending boarding school, she had seen so many students cowed and buckled under the weight of the paparazzo gaze. Every painful, awkward, embarrassing moment pulled out for inspection. And in her darkest nightmares, the moment that her crimes were published for the world to see brought an unimaginable terror to her. Even the thought that they might discover her father's identity, as shielded as it possibly could be, scared her, deepening her dependence on denial. They wouldn't, couldn't find out. She'd worked so hard to separate her life from before from her life now.

But it was precisely these thoughts that prevented her usually quick mind from putting two and two together to understand what any of what Loukis was saying had to do with her.

She looked up at him then, his fierce gaze

studying her intently. The steely line of his jaw, tense, his hands braced as if forewarning her of some life-changing moment.

'What is it?'

'I cannot risk any further damage to my reputation. Not with Annabelle's happiness and future at stake. I *will* not let Meredith get her hands on her, even for a minute.'

She nodded, still not quite understanding where he was going with this.

'Which is why I need you to sign a non-disclosure agreement.'

The statement came as a bit of a surprise to Célia, but she would have been more than happy to agree to such a thing for the happiness of the little girl who had already begun to creep into her heart.

'Is that all?' she asked, half relieved that it seemed to be the case. She took a sip of wine to steady her trembling nerves.

'No. Sadly it is not. What I need of you now, in light of the press article, is your hand in marriage.'

CHAPTER FOUR

FORTY-FIVE SECONDS LATER, Loukis was wiping at the front of his wine-covered shirt and Célia was mortified.

She didn't think that actually happened, she'd honestly only seen it in films. But the moment Loukis had uttered his declaration, the gorgeous mouthful of wine Célia had just taken erupted in a half cough, half gasp that covered Loukis's chest from across the table.

'I'm so... Loukis, I...'

He cut through the air with a free hand, while the other maintained its hasty dabbing and then seemed to give up altogether. A painful blush rose on her cheeks, stinging in its intensity. Her hands were twisting around each other, as if hand-wringing was some age-old inherited act to express... Célia honestly didn't know what to think or to feel about Loukis's strange demand.

With a less than happy sigh, Loukis returned to his seat opposite her as if his five-hundred-dollar shirt had not been ruined and he was clearly determined to resume…negotiations?

'You want to marry me?' Célia asked, unable to prevent the slight trembling from affecting her voice.

'No! *Christos*, no.'

The punctuation of the second denial felt borderline cruel and unnecessary.

'We just have to be engaged, until the court awards me custody.'

Célia felt as if she were playing catch up. 'Why would the court appoint you legal guardian over Annabelle's mother?'

'Because I will prove that she is deeply unsuitable to raise the child she abandoned over three years ago. You've already witnessed the lengths my sister has gone to in order to avoid seeing Meredith, let alone live with the woman.'

Célia couldn't argue with that. Even though it had taken little on her part to distract the young girl, she'd clearly been upset enough to cause a great deal of fear and worry on her behalf.

'But why do you need *me*?'

Loukis looked at her, clearly frustrated that she hadn't just jumped to his demand.

'That photo and the press furore around it will cut through every single inch of positive publicity I have spent the last few years clawing back. I have only two months until the court hearing and there is no time for damage limitation. This, as loath as I am to admit, is the only way to counter the negative impact and present to the court the exact kind of family unit they would need from me in order to grant custody.'

The headache Célia had managed to ward off earlier came back full force and struck her right between the temples. She pressed her thumbs there, ignoring the way that this seemed only to increase Loukis's frustration.

'I'm really not sure this is a good idea. I'm certainly not going to lie to a court judge, Loukis.'

'What would you be lying about? We'd be engaged. That's the truth,' he said with a shrug as if it were that easy.

'I would be lying by telling the judge that we plan to spend the rest of our lives together.'

'No more than any other couple entering into marriage. The road to hell is, after all, paved with good intentions.'

His cynicism regarding the institution was, while not wholly unexpected, painstakingly obvious and for just a moment Célia felt a little sorry for him. And while she understood his attempts to indicate marriage was some form of hell, she didn't think he was so obtuse as to not realise that the same could be said precisely of the endeavour he was suggesting himself.

'And what about Annabelle? What would you

tell her? You can't expect a ten-year-old to lie about something like that, and nor can you expect me to lie to a ten-year-old. Loukis, please,' she begged, 'there must be another way.'

'Oh, yes, absolutely. The other way is for the press to assume that you spent the night with a client. A client with a particularly sordid reputation of seducing and then abandoning all manner of women. I'm sure that would have a beneficial impact on *both* our reputations. I wonder how many charities would want to work with you then?'

Célia felt the colour drain from her face. 'But it could be explained.'

'It could,' he assured her in a tone so insincere her teeth ached. But the tenor of his next statement cast chills across her skin. 'But I have absolutely no intention of doing so. If I'm going down…'

Célia had seen Loukis as many things, but crude and cruel were new to her.

'That's blackmail.'

'Yes.'

His word was swift and assured, contrasting harshly with the threat he had conjured in her mind and the sea of emotions threatening to overwhelm her. For a moment, she was transported back to the last life-defining moment that had pushed her to a precipice she hadn't seen coming. The sickening realisation that she had been used against her will by the very last man she had ever expected it from.

For five years, she had kept her head down, had changed her name to cut all connections with her father, had swapped her university degree, had done everything she possibly could to avoid any kind of spotlight or attention. Instead, she had funnelled her every waking moment into creating a business that would give back...that she hoped would somehow compensate for her naïve actions five years before. The energy and determination that had taken had nearly consumed her. But this time, she couldn't run. This time, she couldn't hide.

Because she believed in her business, had carefully cultivated a rise from the ashes of her previous life. And she would not do that again. So clearly could she see the morning newspaper headlines, she was half convinced they had already happened. Her reputation would be in ruins. Everything she'd worked so hard to achieve, destroyed. By this man. Determination fired in her breast as she fought for control in a situation Loukis currently dominated.

'What do I get out of it?'

'I can pay you,' he said with a shoulder shrug that indicated it was nothing to him. The money, the coercion...

'I don't want your money,' Célia exclaimed with nausea and distaste vying for pole position.

'Then what do you want?'

She shook her head, utterly horrified by their conversation. Was she actually considering this? Could she even do this? Pretend to be his fiancée? She forced her chaotic thoughts into some semblance of order. Her business was her sole focus. It was the only way she could compensate for her past mistakes. The thought of being paid to be draped across his arm was utterly unpleasant. But if it could bring about more help for more charities…

'I want six new clients,' she decided out loud.

Loukis raised his eyebrows. 'Six?'

'If you want to make it ten, then—'

'Six is fine,' he interrupted hastily.

Loukis felt the pressure in his chest build. He was so close. Célia was, at least, considering his proposal. He had no idea where he might find six potential clients, but he would. He couldn't risk letting Célia realise how much power she wielded in that moment. She could ask for the moon and he'd have to make it happen.

'What does it actually entail? I mean, how do you see this playing out?' she asked, her quick mind leapfrogging ahead of his own. He'd been so focused on actually getting her to agree that he didn't have all his plans in place. But Loukis was used to thinking on his feet. He wasn't in charge of one of the world's top ten companies for nothing.

'A very public engagement for at least the next four months. After that, I'm sure we can manage a press announcement that outlines how we have decided to amicably separate.'

'Yes, but what does it actually mean? I have a business in Paris, a life there. I have upcoming events.'

Loukis bit back the scoff of derision. She had only one event, he very much knew that to be the case, but if it gave her the semblance of security to exaggerate her schedule, he would allow her that.

'You would need to relocate to Greece for the duration. We would need to be seen in public as much as possible. There would be an engagement party at least, but I would also be willing to accompany you to the…*events* you have in your diary.'

'How very generous of you,' she said with as much disdain as womanly possible. 'Just like that, you expect me to move to Greece?'

'We will, of course, have been keeping our relationship a secret for the past few months. Not only to protect our privacy, but also your business interests. You were deeply concerned about the effect that this would have on the many fabulous charities you already work with.'

'Was I, now?'

'Are you not?'

'Yes, of course—'

'Then we are simply backdating a few things.'

Her pretty amber eyes flashed ominously.

'It is for your benefit as much as mine, I assure you.' His statement did nothing to dampen the narrowing of her gaze, or the warning it contained. He sighed, resisting the urge to place his head in his hands. 'I will obviously support financially any expenditure generated by this.'

'Oh, that's okay, then. Because of course my first concern was being out of pocket. Not the fact that you want me to lie to the press, a court of law and your little sister.'

'She is the reason I'm doing this. The *only* reason. Her happiness and security are my primary concern. I will find you six new clients. I will ensure that your time in this will not be detrimental to you or your business. I will do everything in my power to make this as seamless and painless as possible. Do you agree?'

'Do I have a choice?'

'Of course you do. If you make the right one, you'll be fine.'

The unspoken threat hung in the air between them. Loukis could honestly say that this was an all-time low, even for him, but he'd not been left with much of the same choice that Célia seemed to desperately want for herself. He held his breath until he saw her head bow and caught her gently muttered agreement.

'Great. I'll have the paperwork drawn up first thing tomorrow morning.'

No ring, no words of love, no undying declaration. Paperwork. A signature. What on earth had she got herself into?

Time seemed to move differently for Célia the moment she had aligned herself with Loukis. As if under his expressive hands it sped up and slowed down, bent to his will.

She hated that he had been right. Right about the reaction from the world's press, the accusatory headlines at first placing a notch beside her name on his bedpost. Then after a very carefully worded release from both his company and Chariton Endeavours, she was scrubbed out, removed from that particular wooden totem, and placed beside his name as some kind of wonder; the woman who had tamed the playboy.

He had also been right about the need for her to leave Paris, where her apartment simply wasn't prepared for the onslaught of nearly one hundred reporters armed with cameras and notepads. Her neighbours had all but requested her removal from the premises, not wholly unreasonably considering hers weren't the only rubbish bags that had been picked through with a fine-tooth comb.

But it was Ella that had surprised her the most. She had expected caution, concern, questions... not the high-pitched squeal of joy Célia put down to post-pregnancy hormones. Somehow she'd wanted Ella just to *know*. To realise that this was beyond Célia's usual behaviour. To understand that there were other forces, namely Loukis Liordis, at play. But Ella had only been full of questions Célia didn't feel equipped to answer. What was their first date like, their first kiss? When did she know he was 'the one'? The fact that none of these things had actually happened suddenly and painfully stuck in Célia's mind.

And then, after the litany of questions, came the deep sigh and, *'I'm so pleased that you've moved on. It's been such a long time since Marc...'*

And that had been too much. Célia had ended the call, disconnecting the painful conversation so much easier than preventing the memories from surfacing.

Because they had surfaced and hung within her all the way through the flight to Greece. The hurt, the confusion...the way, just as everything she'd thought she'd known about herself and her life was shifting, Marc—her last mooring—had removed himself, all the while blaming her.

Which was why, when she arrived back at Loukis's estate just outside Athens, she wasn't prepared for the presence of a small, bespectacled woman, dressed head to toe in black, with a ponytail so severe Célia almost winced in empathy for her hair follicles.

'You see what I'm dealing with?' demanded Loukis, without even looking up at her from where he was furiously typing away on his laptop.

The woman's close scrutiny both up *and* down Célia's entire being was intrusive to say the least.

'I see,' the woman replied, drawing out the second word as if it could convey the gravity of the situation. What situation they were referring to, though, Célia had no idea.

She jumped when the woman approached with a feline grace and began to walk a three-hundred-and-sixty-degree circuit around her. Célia was speechless until the moment the bespectacled woman leaned in to within inches of her face and uttered a low hum.

'What is going on?' Célia demanded. She had always hated such close inspection. In fact, it was precisely why she continued to choose the most unassuming, blandly coloured clothing. She just didn't want to invite that kind of observation.

'Have her to me by three this afternoon.'

Loukis gave a wave of acknowledgement and the woman disappeared.

'Hello, Loukis. It's nice to see you. Yes, my flight was good, thank you for asking. No, I've already eaten and yes, I think I would like something to drink now.'

Finally he looked up, slightly confused.

Only the moment he did, she wished he hadn't. With his hair slightly tousled as if he'd run his hand through it more than once, his shirt loose at the neck…the moment that confusion cleared from his gaze, his eyes hit her like arrows. It was a little too much. She had forgotten the impact that he could make.

She fiddled with her handbag, aware that her few suitcases were being dropped off in the hallway behind her.

'What am I doing at three?' she asked, suddenly uncomfortable with the realisation that she had moved all her portable possessions into the home of Loukis Liordis.

He continued to stare at her as if something was wrong. She frowned, placing a hand against her cheek. Maybe she had something on her face? Finally he turned back to his laptop.

'You're going to a stylist.'

'A what?'

'We're going to be seen in a lot of very exclusive places and I can't have you wandering around in that.' He'd broken off his typing only to gesture to her roughly with one hand in a sweeping circular motion.

'But I—'

'I told you to burn that T-shirt.'

It had been perverse of her to insist on wearing it today, she'd known that. But she hadn't been able to help herself. It was an act of defiance. An act of revenge that for some reason had given her just a little of the strength she'd needed to get onto the plane in the first place.

Until the moment she saw herself through his eyes. Standing in his exquisite Athenian estate where sophistication practically dripped from the modern glass chandelier, beautiful swathes of cream and grey adding a surprising warmth to the impersonal wealth she found herself surrounded by, she felt…uncouth.

But more than that she felt hurt. That familiar sting that she had been found wanting. That once again, she wasn't living up to the perfection people wanted from her. People like her father, Marc, and now Loukis. She knew that Loukis wasn't being personal, but practical. And it shouldn't hurt, but it did. Now the T-shirt just felt petty. All her pride and defiance melted away and she gripped her jaw against the swelling tide of emotion she desperately wanted to put down to jet lag.

She cast about for a distraction. Anything that would remove the microscope from her and onto something new.

'Is Annabelle here?'

'She is in Texas.' His clipped tones as harsh as the sounds of his fingers bashing against the keypad of his laptop.

'Really?' she replied, half fearful and half disappointed that there wouldn't be a natural buffer between her and her new fiancé.

'The visit with Meredith was court appointed. And trust me, I tried to fight it.'

'Is she okay? You've spoken to her?'

Loukis didn't miss the concern in her voice and it touched him. He might not have set out on this path wanting a fiancée, but the fact that Célia, who by unhappy circumstances had unwittingly entered into that role, clearly valued his sister's happiness was a gift.

He just wished that he had more time. More time to get to know Célia, to have vetted her, to have…thought it through a little more? He hadn't invited a woman back to his estate ever. His affairs had been conducted far away from here. And that was *before* Annabelle.

Whatever the press might think, it had been three years since he'd lived up to his playboy reputation. A reputation he'd indulged and enjoyed greatly—as had the women who had graced his bed—until the moment he realised the damage it had done to his future.

But it was the damage from his past that had designed his present. All he had known of marriage had been harshly shouted arguments heard from his hiding place on the staircase. His nights were consumed with them. They would start almost immediately after his bedtime. He would be in that lovely hazy moment of near sleep when they would begin. His father complaining about his mother's drinking, which would escalate to her blaming him for the demise of her modelling career—and by extension Loukis. Then his father would retaliate by raging about her less than private affairs, her extended absence from the family home. On and on, through the nights and years they would go. Throwing verbal barbs and opening wounds, apparently careless of whether their son might be listening.

Marriage, to Loukis, had seemed a battleground. Relationships had become something that he'd never wanted to willingly entertain. Oh, he knew there were instances of couples that seemed to have found their joy in each other. But they were few and far between and dissipated beneath the pain and ferocity of his parents' own relationship.

But, as Célia peered at him from her stance

taken up in the doorway as if ready to bolt at any moment, he reminded himself that he wasn't getting married. That this was a fake engagement to ensure that his sister never bore witness to such a thing. Was never tainted by that same feeling that he had been.

Meredith's abandonment of her three years before had already done enough damage. His sole focus, now, was to ensure that no more harm could be done to his sister.

'I'm due to speak to her later tonight. But she has arrived and is...well. With them.'

'Them?'

'Meredith has apparently found herself a rich Texan oil baron as her latest victim. I can only imagine that the man has strong family values, otherwise Meredith would never have returned for Annabelle. Children—according to my mother—have an aging affect that is deplorable to her.'

He recited the line by rote. One of the many accusations she had hurled at his father.

'I'm sorry, Loukis.'

He must have given himself away. Perhaps his mask had slipped to reveal emotions that were far too close to the surface for his liking.

'My housekeeper will show you to our room. Your bags should already—'

'Our?'

He frowned, wondering what had been unclear about his statement. 'Yes, "our" room.'

He could have laughed at the shocked look on her face, widening her beautiful amber eyes with something akin to horror. That was new. He'd never had that reaction to the suggestion he share a bed with a woman before.

'I'm not sharing a…room with you,' she replied, clearly stumbling over the moment she might have said bed.

Instantly the misstep threw up a riotous display of imagery, Loukis peeling away the straps of her bra, placing kisses across the delicate line of her collarbone, leading down over the gentle slope of her breast to—

Loukis cut off the errant chain of thought, desperately fighting the shocking streak of arousal that had shot through him and instead casting his gaze to the hallway to make sure that no staff were within hearing distance.

'Would you care to sit for this conversation?' he asked, gesturing to the seat opposite him.

'I'll stand, thank you,' she replied, as if waiting, bracing herself for some kind of penance.

'Célia, let me explain something to you. You have agreed to become my fiancée.'

'I don't remember being given much choice.'

'And as such,' he pressed on as if she had not interrupted, 'we need to be seen as a couple very much in love and ready to spend the rest of our lives together. And when I say "be seen", I do not mean just when we're out in public. Everything I have, everything I love, is riding on this engagement being believed. By everyone. By Meredith, by the courts, by my sister and I will not have that at risk because a member of my staff sees that we are using separate rooms.'

Although he had not raised his voice to a level that could be overheard, Célia felt the vehemence of his words right down to her toes. His insistence that they share a room became a primal demand within her, one she seemed powerless to deny.

Célia knew what he was saying made sense. That it was in her interest as much as his not to be found out. Because if they were, the damage to her reputation and business would be apocalyptic. But the thought of sharing a room, let alone a bed, with Loukis Liordis was terrifying. Not because she was in any way scared of the man. No, she was more scared of herself. Because somehow the thought of sharing such an intimacy with him thrilled her. It sent a cascade of electrical bursts through her body, ensuring that every inch of her was hyperaware, over-sensitised even. She hadn't even felt this way about Marc. And that was warning enough.

CHAPTER FIVE

CÉLIA STEPPED OUT of the car that had picked her up from the stylist's and brought her to what she could only presume was one of Greece's most renowned restaurants—if the deluge of supercars on display lining the road was anything to go by. Ferrari, Maserati, Lamborghini, McLaren. The brands rolled off her tongue like a shopping list for the rich and famous.

Reluctantly she had to admit that four hours ago she would have been terrified to even get out of the car. But Layna, despite her severe and frosty demeanour, had been a revelation. Instead of being superior and dismissive, she had peppered Célia with a hailstorm of questions. What she wanted from her clothing, what colours she had in her apartment, did she have a favourite painting, what did she see clothing as being to her. All the different questions had initially seemed unconnected, but as Layna took her through the selection she had cultivated while

Célia was getting her hair and make-up done, she realised how the woman had woven a select wardrobe built from *her*. How each piece reflected something of the answers she had given about her life, her tastes, her fantasies even. She couldn't deny how they flattered and had miraculously unfurled some hitherto unknown sense of pride and satisfaction in her looks.

Which had made her sad. Sad because, once, she had loved dressing in bright clothes, had relished a sense of her own beauty. Before she had cast aside her family name, been discarded by Marc, and hidden within bland, invisible clothing so as not to be seen. Not to be noticed. Because if she was honest with herself, Célia was a little fearful of what such close inspection would reveal.

She brushed aside a layered lock that she was just about getting used to. Before the hair stylist had got his hands on her, she had been unconcerned about the universally shoulder-length, light brown strands. And perhaps that had been part of the problem. The moment she had caught sight of herself in the mirror she hadn't been able to prevent the shocked gasp that had fallen from her lips.

'*Nai.* Good? Good.'

She hadn't even been able to muster any kind of resentment at the knowing gaze and asked and answered question from the hair stylist. Because he was right. Taking her hair a few shades darker, a rich, warm auburn shade of mahogany, had made her somehow more *her*. Her pale skin now seemed creamier, richer. And her eyes— they glowed. She glowed. But more than that, she felt it deep within her. A feminine pride she hadn't realised that she'd sorely missed.

As she got out of the car, she picked up the gorgeous forest-green silk of the dress's skirt so it wouldn't get damaged on the pavement. The moment she had seen the dress, her heart had thudded in her chest. She'd never usually wear such a thing, certainly couldn't usually afford such a thing, but Loukis appeared to be more than willing to fund the extravagance. The dress seemed timeless, having borrowed aspects from different periods, and rather than confusing was somehow eternally elegant. The halter-neck detail that swept from behind her neck, between her breasts and round to the low dip of her spine offered a more risqué design, while the style of the details, the small green jewels sewn into the overlaid cream fabric, suggested grandeur and delicacy.

Her make-up had been kept simple apart from a swipe of bright red matt lipstick and her only accessory was a golden clutch that—as yet—

was completely empty. 'But appearances must be kept,' Layna's command echoing in her mind.

Her golden sparkly heels glinted in the street lights and as she straightened up, she caught the approving glance of the driver, before he quickly masked his features. It fired a little spark within her. Not because of the driver, but because it gave her a little hope as to what Loukis's reaction might be.

And momentarily she faltered, wobbling a little on her too-high heel. She shouldn't be wondering that. She shouldn't be blurring the lines at all. This wasn't some fairy-tale romance, with her own private Cinderella moment. This was a carefully constructed lie in order to get Loukis what he wanted. Hadn't he already proved the lengths he would go to in order to do so? Hadn't he already threatened her reputation and her business? No. She had to remember that he was proving himself to be just like her father, just like Marc. Only interested in her for what she could get for him.

It was precisely this chain of thought that caused the slight flattening of her lips, the barely perceptible tense line to her shoulders. None of the other diners in the restaurant would have noticed such a thing, all too readily consuming the beautiful vision she presented. But Loukis did. He noticed every single thing about her as she walked towards the glass-fronted balcony to where he sat at a table beneath the night sky, waiting but most definitely not ready.

The fierce red slash of colour on her lips was almost carnal and his hands clenched into fists as she swayed towards him provocatively on high-heel-clad feet. Her hair was a different shade, which seemed so much more natural than her previous colouring. The colour reminded him of autumn, but a glorious fireball of autumn that promised warmth…heat even.

Fire. He was playing with fire. Because he couldn't help but acknowledge that he'd found Célia strangely alluring even dressed in that horrible beige top. But that inner sense of beauty he'd known she masked was now on full display for all to see. And it was incredible.

Wordlessly, he stood as the waiter guided her towards him, as if presenting him with some great gift. He watched as she walked towards him. The streak of lightning that cut through him when their eyes met was something he tried hard to ignore. This evening had one purpose. Everything had been arranged, right down to the second. That should be what he was focusing on, not the way that her hips swayed beneath the deep green silk of her dress, the way that it veed down her sternum, revealing rather than hiding the dramatic slope of her breasts. Not the way it cut in at her waist, giving her a true hourglass figure and making his mouth water.

As she reached the table neither seemed capable of moving and, while the waiter discreetly retreated, they faced each other like combatants. Breaking the spell, he rounded the table and pulled out her chair for her, his arms either side of her feeling the heat from her body through the thin linen shirt he wore, his sleeves rolled back so that the fine dark hairs on his arms pricked up. He lingered imperceptibly, pausing just long enough to try to identify the gentle swathe of perfume kissing his senses, one he vaguely remembered from before. It was a bitter-sweet citrus scent that was balanced by something fresh and delicious that reminded him of basil.

He felt her flinch beneath him and removed himself from temptation, skirting back around the table and resuming his own seat. He sighed. No one was going to believe they were engaged if she kept jumping every time he came within a hair's breadth of her.

'Did you—'

'You look—'

They had spoken together and each cut themselves off mid-sentence at the same time. Loukis frowned his discomfort. There was an awkwardness between them that hadn't been present before. But then, before, they'd been working together. Now they were…

He gestured for her to go first.

'Did you manage to get hold of Annabelle?'

Loukis clenched his teeth, not needing to vent his frustrations at this moment in time. He would wait until later for that. 'Meredith had decided to take her out for the afternoon, so I will have to try again later.'

She nodded and looked about. He wondered what she was seeing. The balcony of the restaurant jutted out from the building like an architectural feat, dramatically increasing the floorspace of the flat rooftop. He had reserved the whole area. For privacy and for other important reasons, not least because of the beautiful views of the Athenian skyline at night. Framed by the dark slash of the mountain range, the Parthenon was lit dramatically in the distance, its place high up on the hill drawing every gaze, tourist and local alike. Dusk had fallen, barely an inch of pale purple remaining as the dark promise of night bled into it.

Loukis took this all in in one glance, his gaze reluctant to leave her for more than a few seconds.

'You look beautiful.'

Her amber eyes flew back to him from the horizon, as if she was attempting to silently interrogate his meaning, his motivation.

'Better than the beige T-shirt, then,' she said, the sting of the bitterness in her tone dimmed slightly by the sadness he didn't miss in her eyes.

'The item in question was offensive only in that it was painfully obvious what you were trying to hide.'

'And that was?' she asked, seemingly genuinely intrigued.

'Everything in you that is innately beautiful.'

He hadn't meant to say those words. He hadn't mean to be so truthful. But there was a vulnerability about her that night that called forth the only honesty he could give her.

He knew women well. Had made it his mission to study and understand them when his own mother seemed so impossible to predict, to identify. So he knew women who would hide their pain beneath brittle masks, knew women who displayed their sensuality like a glorious fan of peacock feathers, knew women who aggressively sought dominance where they had once lost it in the past, and knew women who hid their inner sense of power and sensuality, hoarding it protectively from view. And he very much thought that Célia was of the latter variety. But as if sensing it was too much for both of them, he picked up and perused the menu blindly.

'What would you like to drink?'

As if the waiter had sensed it was safe to return, he appeared on the balcony to take their order.

Célia seemed to take a deep breath, turned smilingly at the man and ordered a martini. It surprised him; her choice bold, the drink dry, and the request for a twist of lemon rather than an olive seemed to suit her.

'Same,' he stated to the waiter without taking his eyes off Célia, who was clearly uncomfortable with his constant gaze.

'I'm surprised that you didn't order for me,' she said, placing her hands on her lap beneath the table. Probably, he assumed, turning them within each other as she had done before.

'That was for speed and efficiency. This is not.'

'What is this for, then?'

It was then that he decided not to tell her of his plans for that evening. He would need her to be as natural as possible—and even before they had ordered drinks she'd had a streak of tension through her as if she were ready to bolt.

'This is so that we can get to know each other a little more.'

'Is that necessary?' she asked, still unable to meet his gaze.

He reached across the table and placed his

hand on her neck to cup her jaw. As expected she almost jumped right off the chair. But he kept his hand in place, feeling the flickering of her pulse, smoothing it slightly with a swipe of his thumb that caused a sensation within him that he had to fight to temper.

'It is if you're going to stop jumping every time I touch you. We're supposed to be...we *are* engaged. And we're going to have to start acting like it. So,' he said, finally removing his hand, 'I have a game of sorts for us to play.' He waited for her to take this in. 'You will ask a question, and for each one I answer, I will touch you.'

The look of fear that crossed her face bit him hard. 'Not like that, not...' He shook his head, trying to find the words. Where was his usual charm? Where was the man reported to have seduced women in their hundreds? 'We're in public, Célia, it's not as if I'm going to ravish you. Consider it the opposite of aversion therapy. For every question of mine that *you* answer, you will touch me.'

Célia's heart thudded in her chest, her cheek still warm from where he had caressed her. She knew that he was right, that she had to stop being so... overly sensitive to his touch. They would have to put on a performance in public eventually. And out here, beneath the night sky, where the air was warm and there was no one to see them, was surely a safe place to…to…

'You agree?' he cut through her thoughts and she nodded her assent even as she feared what his first question might be.

'What is your favourite colour?'

She laughed then. At the ridiculousness of his question, of her fear. Couldn't help but catch the way his lips had quirked up in a smile as if he'd expected her reaction.

'Orange.'

'Really?'

'Yes,' she laughed.

He nodded, as if impressed somehow. 'I thought it would have been—'

'Don't you dare say it,' warning him away from saying beige.

'*Entáxei*—okay.' His eyes were lit with mischief and the laughter on the air between them had broken some of the tension that had built since she'd first felt the heat from his body as he held out a chair for her.

Loukis laid his arm on the table, his palm outstretched for her, challenging her.

She stared at it as if it were something strange and new. An inexplicable urge took over her then. The desire to touch, to feel, to know… She pressed her thumb into the palm of his hand and drew it upwards along the length of his middle finger, his palm curling in gently as if wanting to prolong their connection, her touch. His skin felt smooth and warm beneath hers and it sent little starbursts across her hand and forearm. She resisted the urge to shiver.

'Your turn,' he said, breaking the spell that had held her in silence.

Her mind strangely blank, she searched for something as bland and unchallenging as the question he had posed, not quite ready to delve deeper.

'What is your favourite food?'

'Baklava.' He answered too quickly for it to be a lie.

'Really?'

'I'm Greek. It would be criminal for me to say otherwise.'

Célia couldn't help but smile at the prideful, playful tone and the trace of starlight in his eyes.

Hesitantly she placed her arm out the way that he had done and laid her hand open on the table before him. It was then that she realised what he had done. That in allowing her to be the one to touch him first, he had ensured that she would not be subjected to anything he wouldn't receive himself. It made her feel…strangely safe. Until he touched her.

Receiving exactly the same touch that she had given sent sparks down her arm to her core, unable this time to prevent the shiver that wracked her body. Her palm flared then curled beneath his finger, just as his had done. Her nipples drew to stiff peaks as arousal, swift and sharp, pierced her and she flinched, withdrawing her hand suddenly.

He masked it quickly, but she saw something pass his features. Frustration, she thought, disappointment perhaps.

'I'm sorry.'

'Don't be. That's why we're doing this. We need to become accustomed to each other,' he stated simply as if he had not been devastated in the same way as she had by something so basic as one touch.

'My turn. Where did you go to school?'

Célia's body spun within some strange vortex as she forced herself to answer the question. 'Switzerland. With Ella. Boarding school.'

'Not France?' he queried, probing for more details.

'No, my fa— My parents wanted me to go to "the best of schools",' she said, adopting her father's imperious tone. She cast a glance to Loukis, and if he noticed the slip, he was kind enough not to press.

He placed his arm on the table again, but this time face down. She hesitated again, then steeled herself for the impact, knowing what to expect this time. She placed her hand over his, smoothing her way up over his wrist and forearm, her fingers dipping beneath the rolled-up shirtsleeves, all the while braced against the sensations that drenched her.

Questions came and answers went, each time eliciting a touch here, there, an elbow, a little finger hooked around another, a thumb, a hand held, and a palm kissed gently. Loukis had moved his chair next to hers, so that the table no longer lay between them. Small plates of delicious food went ignored as the awareness and knowledge of each other deepened.

'What three things would you save in a fire?' Célia finally asked.

'Annabelle.'

Célia smiled. 'That's just one thing,' she chided.

'I don't need anything else.'

His answer struck her more deeply, more viscerally than any other from that night. And suddenly she feared him asking her the same question. Feared that she wouldn't be able to answer it because she didn't have anyone to take with her like that. Anyone who was enough. Belongings seemed insipid in comparison to his answer, the items in her apartment only five years old, nothing from before. Nothing from her childhood. Because in the last five years, she realised, she'd made herself an island. New, shiny, determined, but unanchored, untethered.

Loukis seemed not to realise that she hadn't taken her due, hadn't touched him in turn, because he pressed on with his next question.

'Why do you dress the way you do? What are you hiding from?'

His head was bent towards her as if listening to her unspoken response. *Everything*, she mentally replied, shocking herself. Inexplicably as thoughts of her father's betrayal, of Marc's desertion, of the absence of her mother from her present life rose up around her and she felt the hot press of tears gathering at the corners of her eyes.

Loukis reached up a thumb and gently swept away a tear that had escaped. The warmth and comfort of his palm against her cheek, this time so much more familiar, so much more wanted than earlier in the evening. His face was so close, the lips that had pressed into her hand, her wrist to answered questions, tempting her, teasing her, making her want them, making her want him.

Her heart pounded, crying and demanding for what he was so clearly willing to offer.

Breath left her lungs in defeat as she closed the distance between them, giving up the fight, which she had known would only end one way. Her supplication and his dominance.

The moment his lips met hers, her mind

stopped. Thoughts were lost beneath the heady indulgent sensations of his mouth across hers, his tongue gently sweeping, asking and gaining entrance.

A need, shocking in its intensity, reared in her breast. *More.* She wanted more. Her hands rose to either side of his face, needing to touch, to explore. Her fingers threaded through the fine strands of his hair, relishing the softness, at the same time as riding a wave of something inexplainable, something almost euphoric.

A bright white flash cut through her closed eyes, startling her. Again and again it popped, causing her to rear back in shock.

Eyes wide, mouth thoroughly kissed, Loukis had never seen anything so beautiful, before something like fear covered Célia's features. Even though he'd known it was coming, he'd still felt the intrusion of the paparazzi's flashbulb. The photographs he'd assured would be taken, now unwanted and frustrating.

It was then that he realised that his bright idea, the one that would cement their engagement publicly and assuredly, was a mistake. He saw it as Célia would see it. A betrayal. But as his conscience lashed at him, his need to win, his need to secure custody of Annabelle over Meredith rose hard and fast.

He swiped his lower lip with the pad of his thumb, sure that some of her lipstick had transferred from her mouth to his. As he looked down at the red mark on his skin, he wondered just how badly he had wounded her this evening.

He pushed up out of his chair, ignoring the way that Célia stared out into the distance trying to find the invisible photographer who had caught them in such an intimate, private moment.

'What do we do?' she asked, her voice trembling in the same way that her body had beneath his.

'We leave.'

He placed a guiding arm around her and ushered her from the rooftop, back into the dimly lit interior of the busy restaurant. It seemed impossible to him that there had been upwards of one hundred people on the other side of the glass. He guided her through the tables, noticing the way her skin had become cold, goosebumps pebbled her arms, where previously soft warmth had been all he could feel.

As he stopped by the small desk to the right of the entrance, passing over his credit card, the manager looked up. 'Did you get what you need?'

'Nai,' Loukis said, swiftly cutting off anything further the man might give away. He felt, from where his arm was still placed around Célia, her body stiffen.

As he stalked from the restaurant towards the bank of elevators in the hallway, her footsteps slowed, her face transforming from confusion to disgust.

'What did he mean?'

'I'm sure that he meant to ask if we enjoyed our meal.'

'I don't think so. If that were the case, he would have used those words.'

Something horrifyingly like guilt lashed at him.

'What was it that you needed from this evening, Loukis?' she demanded.

The elevator doors swung open and he stepped inside, studiously ignoring her question.

'What, you no longer want to play your game?' she said, her voice hoarse with emotion as the doors closed behind her.

He inhaled, his mind a swarm of thoughts all the while he could still taste her on his tongue, her scent wrapping around him in the small enclosed space.

She pushed him then, double handed, shocking and no less than he deserved.

'Answer me!'

'I needed the press to have a photograph of us together. I needed us to be seen as a couple,' he growled through clenched teeth, the answers insipid and unsatisfying even to his own ears. 'It needed to seem natural. It had to be perfect.'

'But you didn't have to lie to me. You didn't need to set up some silly game just to get me to...' She seemed unable to bring the words to lips that he'd so thoroughly kissed. He watched her bring herself under control, tried to avoid the way her chest pressed against the silk lining of the dress as she levelled her breathing.

'No more lies, Loukis. I won't be lied to again.'

And something in her tone spoke of more than just his actions that evening. Something deeper and darker. But he refused to delve into it, no matter how much he might want to ask who had hurt her. He had done enough for now.

CHAPTER SIX

LOUKIS RAN A weary hand through his hair as his eyes focused on the bright laptop screen glowing like some unworldly portal in the dark room. He checked the time on the watch on his wrist. Two forty-five in the morning. Anger was keeping him awake. Anger, frustration and an unhealthy dose of discomfort swirled in his empty stomach. He now regretted not touching any of the delicious morsels that had been presented to him and Célia earlier in the restaurant.

In the car on the way home, he had messaged his housekeeper and given her a few days off, realising that there was no earthly way he could make good on his demand that Célia share his bed.

He might be many things, but crass was not one of them.

A few days would give them time to…adjust to one another. But by the time Annabelle was safely back from Texas and away from the clutches of his mother, there would most definitely have to be a united front.

He checked his watch again. Time had slowed to almost imperceptible increments as he waited for the moment when he could video call his sister. And after that, he would collapse into one of the spare rooms upstairs and hope that sleep would somehow dull the way that the evening loomed in his mind. It had taken on a technicolour quality, the vivid slash of Célia's red lipstick, the forest-green silks of her dress, the impact of their kiss still vibrating through him like earthquake tremors long after the fact.

He didn't regret his decisions that evening. The paparazzo was as necessary as getting to know and getting used to Célia. But just when their game had turned from one of necessity to one of expectation, want even, he couldn't tell. And even now he wondered at the answer to the question he had not had time to ask her. What Célia would have saved in the fire.

The screen of his laptop changed as Annabelle's video call appeared, the sudden pings echoing loudly, intrusively in the quiet estate. He grabbed a quick mouthful of cold coffee and accepted the call.

'Hey, Nanny,' he said, using the nickname they'd had for the last three years. Where or how it had come about forgotten beneath the impact of those first few months. 'Have a Texan accent yet?'

Her face filled the screen, bright, shining and happy. She was clutching a bright, torrid-pink fluffy bear, and Loukis's first thought was, *And so it begins*. The buying of Annabelle's affection would have been Meredith's first and obvious move.

'Don't be silly,' she laughed.

'And who have you got there?'

'His name's Jameson.'

'Jameson? That's an interesting name. I like his fur.'

Célia woke up, startled and unable to tell where she was or what had woken her. Her heart was pounding and a thin sheen of salty dampness was rapidly drying in the cool room. Loukis. The photographer. The kiss… All these things seemed to crash down in her mind.

It needed to seem natural. It needed to be perfect.

The word had sliced through her like a knife. *Perfect*. It had been too close. Too reminiscent of Marc, of her father. It was supposed to be different with Loukis. They had an agreement. She knew the terms. And now he did too. *No more lies*. She just had to hope that she could live up to her end of the bargain. To be the one thing that she had failed at before. To be…perfect.

Her mouth was bone-dry and she knew she'd not be able to go back to sleep now. She shrugged on her new silk robe and, on bare feet, made her way towards the staircase that led downstairs.

A sound pulled her up short. Startling and rich, Loukis's laughter cut through her. It was conspiratorial in a way that made her jealous. Perhaps he was on the phone to his lover. And she suddenly felt horrified. They'd never talked about that, and why wouldn't he have one? He was clearly a deeply sensual man—but he'd kissed her? She rubbed her forehead, her thoughts chaotic after an unsettled brief bite of sleep.

In a fit of unfamiliar pique, she continued down the stairs, not disguising her footfalls on the cool marble. She rounded the bottom of the staircase and saw Loukis through the doorway to the living room, illuminated in the darkness by a shaft of light from his laptop screen.

The moment she heard Annabelle's voice echo through the speakers, she felt guilty. Guilty and intrusive. She made to retreat, but the move must have caught his eye, because Loukis looked up, a smile lighting his features momentarily. And then, as if he too remembered how they had left things, how she had stormed off to the room and slammed the door shut on him as if she were a child, the brightness of his smile dimmed.

'Who's that?' she heard Annabelle demand.

Almost reluctantly he beckoned her over and Célia, unable to refuse the command, went to stand behind where Loukis sat so that she could see the screen.

'Bonsoir, ma chérie,' Célia greeted the ten-year-old, expecting and receiving the peal of giggles that the girl emitted.

'She calls me Cherry,' she cried to Loukis in delight.

'You're getting quite the collection of names, Nanny. I hope you can keep track of them,' Loukis said, jokingly chiding.

'Mummy calls me Annabelle, though.'

She felt Loukis jerk back in the chair as if struck.

'But mynewdaddy—' she seemed to roll the words into one '—calls me Anna. He's silly.'

Her statement hit the room with the force of a tornado Annabelle couldn't even have imagined.

'Your new daddy?' Loukis demanded, his voice shaking with anger.

Annabelle looked uncertain for a moment. 'That's what Mummy calls him. My new daddy,' she replied, as if confused and unsure as to why Loukis's reaction was what it had been.

'Are you having fun?' Célia rushed on, trying to cover his discomfort. 'What have you been up to?'

As Annabelle chatted away about visits to

shopping malls, where she was given Jameson, and a trip to the zoo, where she saw tigers, bears and snakes—her favourite was Diego the skunk—Célia was painfully aware of the tension and frustration that filled the air on this side of the world, Annabelle thankfully oblivious to it. Or at least she had been until her voice trailed off a little and her small fingers started to twist in the bright pink fake fur of her toy.

'But I… I… They don't have dolphins. Not like the zoo in Greece.'

Célia's heart ached. For Annabelle and Loukis, both desperately trying to navigate this new dynamic.

'I don't think I've ever seen a dolphin,' she remarked into the awkward silence.

'You haven't?' Eyes wide and childishly outraged, Annabelle demanded that Loukis take her to see the dolphins *right now.*

'*Ma chérie*, it is nearly three-thirty in the morning. I don't think the zoo is open here yet.'

'But it's still light outside?'

'Not here, my love. You're so far away that the sun is in a different place and it's a different time. What are you doing tomorrow?' Célia asked, trying to get some of the happy enthusiasm that had filled the little girl's voice. But sadly it didn't quite work. Her joy was as dimmed as Loukis.

'How is Meredith treating you?' he demanded, his voice rough and begrudging.

'She wants me to call her Mummy.'

All the man beside her could do was nod.

'Is that okay with you?' asked Célia, keeping her tone as light as possible.

Annabelle narrowed her eyes, the weight of the question being given serious consideration.

'I think so?' She darted a look towards Loukis as if to check that she had the right answer and, once again, Célia's heart ached just a little more.

'You call her what feels right for you, *oui*?'

'Wee? Why did you say *wee*?' Annabelle cried, pealing off into another beautiful giggle.

'It is how I say yes,' Célia explained with a smile.

'You talk funny,' Annabelle accused.

'You have funny friends,' Célia replied, pointing to Jameson.

'He *is* funny. And silly. And pink!' she exclaimed.

After a few more minutes, Loukis too quiet to be able to continue pointless conversation, they agreed to video call again tomorrow and signed off.

When Loukis closed the laptop's screen, the living room was shrouded in a sudden darkness that left spots dancing in the backs of Célia's eyes and a weight against her chest that burned.

She understood why Loukis was so angry, but also was frustrated that he'd revealed some of that anger to Annabelle. She was a ten-year-old child and shouldn't bear the weight of adult emotions. Not when she'd soon have enough of her own to deal with.

'What?' Loukis demanded in the darkness. 'I can practically feel the waves of your disapproval.'

'I… It's not my place,' she said, turning to leave the room.

Loukis leaned forward and switched on the lamp beside the laptop, the shaft of light cutting off her escape.

'Well, as my fake fiancée for now, you might as well spit it out.'

She turned back to him, as if reluctant. Her eyes large, glowing and wary as if she knew what she had to say would hurt him. Loukis almost laughed at himself then. *Christos.* What was it with the women in his life?

'It's just a shame, Loukis, that's all. I know you have a complicated relationship with your mother, but Annabelle looked like she was having fun.'

The silent accusation that he might have somehow taken away that fun cut him deep. Meredith was the danger, not him. He was doing everything in his power to protect his sister. And if that protection came at the cost of being spoiled rotten by a flaky woman whose only claim to motherhood was birth, then so be it.

'Oh, fun. Yes, I remember "fun" Meredith,' he bit out. Because he did. He remembered the mother who would arrive at the school, middle of the day sometimes, and whisk him away to the beach, on a yacht, or a trip to the zoo, or to shops full of the best toys. He remembered the way his room had filled with useless presents designed to prove her occasional affections, to make up for the rest of the time. He remembered a woman he thought had hung the moon and more, who made him feel as if he were the only other person in the world. Until something brighter and shinier came along to distract her. Usually a man other than her husband, with more money than sense, who might or might not have owned an island, or a villa in a different part of Greece, or even Europe. Then, he wouldn't see her for weeks. Her absence marked only by a new toy.

'But I also remember the Meredith who would leave me waiting in a playground for three hours before my father could come and get me. Not just once, Célia. Nearly once a week. I remember the Meredith who was too busy enjoying the delights of the Riviera to return for Christmas. Not just the day, the whole damn holiday. I remember the woman who walked out on her daughter one day and never looked back, until now. I remember the nights, weeks, months of Annabelle crying herself to sleep, asking where her mother was and why she wasn't coming back. It was nearly a year before she stopped asking after Meredith. And what do you think will happen to Annabelle, how do you think she'll feel, when Meredith tires of her returned plaything, and wants to drop her off again and disappear? What will Annabelle remember then?'

His voice had grown louder and harsher throughout and he realised he was shaking with anger. Anger for Annabelle, anger for himself, and anger towards Célia, who had only pointed out something he had already been castigating himself for.

He couldn't bear to look at her, fearing and resenting that she had called forth such blatant vulnerability from him. He never spoke about his mother, never spoke about his memories of her. She had left and not once looked back. Not even for his father's funeral. So he had wiped her from his mind, cut her from his life as ruthlessly as a surgeon removing dangerous cells from the body.

He felt Célia's hand on his, and this time it was his turn to flinch. And just as he had done in the restaurant, Célia maintained the delicate contact between them, adding to it even, as she reached for his chin to guide his gaze to hers.

'I am sorry that happened to you.' The sincerity in her gaze scoured. It scoured because in some ways having her understand, having her apology, opened up the hurt in a way it had not been before. Desperate to stifle it, to shove the lid back down hard, Loukis turned back to where the laptop was open on his desk.

'But what if Meredith does actually want a relationship with Annabelle? What if she *does* want to be part of her life? Is that not worth exploring, even if just a little?'

Loukis couldn't help the bitter laugh that escaped at her naivety. 'That woman isn't capable of thinking of anyone else but herself.'

'That's possible. Even likely, given what you've shared. But...'

He was getting tired of trying to sift through her words to find the heart of what she meant. He both wanted and feared her spelling it out, because if he was honest, he thought he might know what she was about to say.

'Just say it, Célia.'

'She will need to make her own mind up, Loukis. She will need to figure out her own feelings about Meredith. And you need to be a safe space for that. You *need* to be non-judgmental as she works through it, because if you don't then you'll be the one creating the wall between you and her, not her and Meredith. If Annabelle's mother is as bad as you say, she'll reveal herself and it will devastate your sister. And she will need you for that.'

He met her statement with the clenched jaw of someone who knew he was in the wrong and she was in the right.

'But your reaction is totally normal. You're acting just like any other parent going through a custody battle.'

'I'm not a parent,' he ground out.

'Really?' she asked, her head to one side as if inspecting him for a deeper truth. 'You are looking to be granted full custody of a child you have spent three years feeding, housing, clothing and caring for and you deny that you're a parent? If not for that, then why are you doing this? Because, Loukis, if you're doing this just to get back at your mother then…'

Then you are just as bad as her.

The unspoken accusation hung in the air between them, a bell that had tolled its tale and rippled out into his consciousness. He shook his head against her words, trying to dislodge the barb that had hooked into his mind.

'I'm going to bed,' she said gently before leaving the room. He barely acknowledged her departure.

Was Célia right? Really? Was it vengeance driving him to seek custody of Annabelle, because of his own hurt feelings, teaching Meredith a lesson perhaps? Or had he told the truth, that his sole motivation was to protect his sister?

In the dimly lit living room, in a chair that after four hours was uncomfortable, he tried out each different chain of thought, listening to his mind and heart as he felt his way through the morass of his motivations. Reluctantly, Loukis was forced to admit that perhaps it was an unsettling mixture of both. But Célia was right. He had to make sure that he kept his own feelings for his mother out of it. Because Meredith would reveal herself soon enough and the blow to Annabelle would be devastating. Not that it stopped his plans for even a second, Loukis decided. He could at least hope to limit that damage by gaining sole custody and ensure that any interaction with Meredith was kept to a minimum.

The next morning, Loukis surprised her. Not only had he, himself, laid out a breakfast of delicious treats, hot and very strong coffee, but he also appeared to be in a good mood.

After the awkwardness from the night before, it was taking Célia a little longer to adjust to this new, charming fiancé. A dull thud hit her heart as she thought of the word. It hadn't been the first time that she'd had a near-fiancé. The word conjured images not of Loukis, but of Marc. Of how charming he'd appeared at first, how joyful and exuberant. All things that had disappeared the moment she'd rejected her father's name, money, and her own burgeoning technical career.

Torn between memories of the past and an unsettling present, it took her a while to realise that Loukis had said something. Or asked something? Because he was looking at her for an answer to some unheard question.

'I'm sorry, what was that?'

Loukis pushed aside the newspaper and leaned forward. Not before she'd got a look at the large black and white photo of them kissing on the rooftop of the balcony the night before. A headline, she was sure, screamed the news of their engagement and apparent happiness. An article, she was equally sure, dredged up the many references to Loukis's past conquests and more questions about who this strange woman who had claimed him was.

'Would you?'

'Would I what?' she asked, irrationally irritated.

'Would you like to go into Athens this morning?' he repeated pleasantly and frustratingly without…well, frustration.

'Oh. Yes, I suppose?'

'You don't seem sure.'

'Loukis, right now, to be honest, I'm not quite sure of anything. Why would we go into Athens?'

His answer surprised her. Silencing her. Making her suddenly a little fearful. Because his answer, his apparent purpose, was their engagement ring. A ring that would make all this so much more tangible. It would draw a line beneath the way she had been trying to pass this whole endeavour off as something not quite real.

Loukis's cheerful mood seemed to carry on through the morning. The journey into Athens in a chauffeur-driven town car had been full of twists and turns that only served to exacerbate the nausea building in her stomach. The Acropolis loomed high in the distance as they drew closer and closer to the city centre. Sleek buildings bordered the road as they wound through the streets, until they came to the sprawling sandstone building housing the Greek Parliament. It rose on one side of the car, large, proud but strangely removed of some of the pomp and finery of other countries' central government. It struck her as both beautiful and uncompromising. A little like the man beside her.

It was soon left in the rear-view mirror as the car took them further into the centre, smaller streets full of motorbike riders risking their lives swerving in and out of traffic, tourists doing much the same as they navigated the busy pavements and side streets. The limousine, drawing curious glances from pedestrians, drew to a halt at the corner of a street, and with lithe grace Loukis exited the car and came round to open her door for her.

It seemed to Célia that these small gestures, manners, were automatic for him and in some ways she preferred that. They weren't intended to ingratiate, there was no purpose to them other than it was simply what he did. It seemed doubtful that this was something his mother had imparted, but more likely that it had been his father. It was on the tip of her tongue to ask, but as she stepped out into the sunlight her mind halted beneath the incredible sight of a riotous waterfall of fuchsia bougainvillea. It was pouring from one side of street, clinging impossibly to a yellow-painted wall, as if challenging the white wisteria blooming forth from the opposite building. It was such a beautiful sight, she couldn't help but smile.

Even at ten in the morning, the street was bustling with people and tourists, and they soon had to step out of the way of the oncoming wave of pedestrians. The trees created a canopy above tables set out on stone-paved streets full of people with coffee and cigarettes and the hum of conversations drifted towards them.

Loukis seemed content to allow her to take her fill of the surroundings.

'You've not been to Athens before now?'

She looked up, smiling, and shook her head. 'I only flew in before for the gala and...well, was gone first thing in the morning, as you know.'

Momentarily his espresso rich coloured eyes darkened, before he schooled his features back to that practised smile and slipped on a pair of sunglasses.

'Come,' he commanded, his hand outstretched to hers. 'We have an appointment.'

She hesitated, momentarily cast back to the feel of his touch, of his kiss from the night before. The aching realisation that their intimacy was for public display returned and she sadly took his hand, chiding herself for the errant thought that she'd wished, for a moment, for him to take her hand because...because he just wanted to.

He led her up the gently sloping street, past restaurants and shops selling everything from ceramic masks of Greek mythology with impressive swirling beards, to leather sandals, and Grecian-style dresses of turquoise, white and fuchsia. The bright vibrancy was infectious and soon smoothed away most of the exhaustion from the night before.

She was thankful, as the heat of the sun began to warm the streets, that she had determinedly chosen her clothing from her new wardrobe. The wide-cut tan linen palazzo trousers and white T-shirt, more fitted that she would usually have worn, were a godsend. Loukis, too, was in linen, dark trousers and a white shirt, rolled back at the sleeves, with his jacket hooked on his finger and trailing over his shoulder. He looked every inch the charming playboy and for the first time she felt as if she might just fit in beside him.

They drew to a halt at a small building squashed between two others, one a restaurant and another selling antique books. The darkened windows looked closed to further inspection, but Loukis confidently ushered her through the door before him.

A small man who could not be any younger than eighty greeted Loukis like a long-lost friend, taking him by the arms in a deceptively strong grip and kissing both cheeks of her soon-to-be official fiancé.

A smattering of Greek filled the small room, which, as her eyes adjusted, she could see was absolutely full of the most incredible jewellery. Shafts of sunlight from the street picked out princess-cut diamonds, baguette cuts of what looked like blue tourmaline, pear-shaped rubies far out-shining the cluster of tiny pearls in which they were set…it was as if she'd wandered into Aladdin's cave.

As the two men continued to chat away, Célia's eyes snagged on a marquise-cut diamond solitaire. A whisper of hurt wound out from her heart. It was exactly like the ring Marc had once pointed out to her.

'When I ask your father for your hand in marriage, that is the ring I will buy you.'

At the time, she'd been so overwhelmed, thought she'd been so happy, she hadn't realised that his 'proposal' had been more of a statement, and that he'd put her father first. The signs had all been there, she just hadn't wanted to see them.

'Really?'

Loukis's question interrupted her thoughts.

'*That* is what's caught your eye?'

'I was just looking. You don't like it?'

'It's not whether I like it, but it doesn't quite seem like you.'

How was it that this man, who she barely knew, who she had yet to even share a bed with, seemed to know her better than Marc, with whom she had spent nearly four years?

'What do you think would suit me best, then?' she asked, pushing past her bruised and battered heart.

He levelled her with a gaze so considered she wanted to turn away, fearful that he might somehow divine her thoughts. Finally, as if deciding something, he took her by the shoulders and guided her to a velvet ring display on top of the counter. The old man stood behind it with an exhilarated look across his features. She was distracted by that for a moment, before looking down at the single ring held by the dark velvet folds.

'Oh.' She couldn't have prevented the small sound of shock falling from her lips. It was beautiful; a thin gold band, set with bright green sapphires in a half eternity pattern. It was everything that she would have ever wanted for her engagement ring. And it was altogether too much.

The man behind the counter gently prised the ring from where it lay and gave it to Loukis, gesturing for him to present it to his fiancée.

'I'm sure it won't…'

She trailed off as Loukis took her hand in his, his thumb unfurling her ring finger, smoothing away the slight tremors she felt across her skin, and slid the exquisite piece down to where it fitted, perfectly at the base of her finger.

She looked up at him then. She shouldn't have, but she couldn't resist. The look in his eyes, the dark promise, the undercurrent of something more than just an agreed upon fake relationship, shocking them both.

CHAPTER SEVEN

As Loukis exited the shop, he tried to ignore the residual feelings that had been brought on the moment he slipped the engagement ring onto Célia's finger. For a man who had been determined to avoid such a thing ever happening, he put it down to the fact he was going against his very nature. Rather than the fact that for a moment, in the shop, Célia had seemed utterly vulnerable. Without artifice or defence, her expressive amber eyes had contained too much. Had communicated too much.

He grasped her hand and placed his arm around her shoulders, persevering through the flinch he had expected, and settled her into his side, careless of the other pedestrians trying to rush around them in their haste.

He felt her head scan to one side, then the next, as much as he saw it from his peripheral vision, given that she barely reached his shoulder.

'What are you looking for?' he asked, curious.

'The press. Surely you wouldn't want them to miss this moment.' The bitterness on her tongue was harsh, but just.

'No press. Not today.'

'Giving me the day off?'

'I think you've deserved it,' he said, trying to keep his voice light. 'What would you like to do now?'

'I get a say in the matter, do I?'

He was beginning to get more than a little frustrated, so he drew her around to face him.

'Célia.'

'I know. I'm sorry, it's just all a bit too much.'

'Which is why I wanted today to be fun.'

She huffed out a laugh. 'Fun?'

'Yes, you do remember fun, don't you?' Although looking at her reaction, perhaps she didn't. 'How long have you been working on Chariton?'

She inhaled, the action tempting his gaze to her breasts, but he resisted. Barely.

'Three years, give or take. Ella and I were talking about it long before, when we were still at university.'

'When was the last time you had a holiday? Or just took a break?'

That she avoided both his gaze and his question told him enough. He sneaked an arm around her waist and guided her back up the street.

'Where are we going?'

'First we are going to Monastiraki, which has a flea market perfect for our purposes of simply enjoying the morning. Then we have lunch.'

Loukis had decided not to tell Célia about the lunch meeting he had arranged for her. He'd not missed the way that, if given too much time to think, Célia would over prepare, over question and over doubt. When she met the first prospective client he had arranged, as agreed upon as part of the fake fiancée deal, Loukis wanted her to be as natural as possible.

She dragged her heels for a while, but soon relaxed, guided by his arm around her shoulder, Loukis telling himself the touch was necessary for them both. Aversion therapy, he had said the night before. The problem was that Loukis was not in the least averse to touching her.

The smell of strong coffee and sweet treats filled the air, his mouth watering at expectation of the honey and pistachio of a baklava. As if Célia was having the same thoughts, her footsteps slowed, and he smiled.

'Coffee? Baklava?'

She nodded, smiling, and they took a seat at one of the free tables out in the street. Dappled light picked out shadows on the white tablecloth as it filtered through the leaves above. The warmth of early summer comforting. He loved

Athens at this time of year. A little too early for the massive influx of tourists that would usually drive him and Annabelle from their estate out to the island. It had been the first property he'd ever bought. Somewhere that his mother hadn't tainted, his father's devastation hadn't touched, and where he initially and then, later, Annabelle had both found a peace…no. More than that. They had—for a while—found happiness. Suddenly, without warning, the looming custody battle set his heartbeat racing as he vainly tried to struggle with the fear, shocking and terrible, that he might lose Annabelle.

The waiter came with menus, but Loukis waved them away, simply ordering baklava, an espresso for himself and *frappe metrio* for Célia. He thought she would like the sweet iced coffee. As the waiter disappeared back into the restaurant, his attention was drawn by a father and son on the nearby table. The son was angrily wiping at his eye with one hand, as if trying to disguise his tears, and holding what looked like a small black electronic plane in the other.

He heard the father's reassurances, and almost felt the man's helpless anger as he tried to explain to the boy that there must be something wrong with it. That they just had to wait until they could go back to the shop. Though judging from the look on the father's face, he either didn't hold out much hope for a solution or feared the money it would cost. Loukis empathised with the man, clearly struggling with his child's hurt and pain. Since Annabelle had come into his life, he'd felt that constantly.

Célia turned to look behind her, her gaze seeming to snag on the same tableaux as his had done.

'What's wrong?'

Loukis shook his head, shrugging. 'Something wrong with the machine apparently.'

He watched as she cocked her head to one side as if trying to get a closer look at the machine, rather than the boy and his father, which struck him as a little odd. She shifted her chair a little, so she could better see, which drew the attention of the upset little boy and his father.

'Can you ask him what's wrong with it?' she said to Loukis.

Frowning, he relayed the question and the father's answer, all three of them looking rather bemused by Célia's interest.

She nodded, and held her hand out for the toy.

The boy looked to his father for permission and, once granted, passed the machine over to Célia.

It felt strange having a drone in her hands again. Strange, exciting, sad…a heady combination as she placed the lightweight black body on her lap and scrolled through the controller to switch the language from Greek to French. She was familiar with the cheap mass-produced brand—a family favourite that entertained children and adults alike. Checking that the drone was powered up, she scrolled to the status bar to find the compass setting. She had already checked the aircraft battery was above eighty per cent, so she was pretty sure that recalibrating the compass should be all that was needed. Looking for the solid clear light at the back of the drone, she put the controller aside, and picked up the body of the machine, turning it in her hands three hundred and sixty degrees until the light ran green. Pointing the nose downwards, she turned the machine again until the green light started flashing. Which was just as it should be.

She looked up at the boy, smiling, and passed him back the drone and controller after switching the language back to Greek.

The boy took it from her gingerly, placed it on the ground and experimentally started the drone up. It jerked upwards, startling some passers-by, and the boy let out a cry of joy, before guiding it up and into the air, running a short way after it.

For a moment, she indulged. Indulged in her own childhood memories. The hours she had spent playing with similar toys, and then later, the years she had spent studying, working towards more and more complex designs, GPS systems, loving the way that binary numbers combined with computer chips and the smell of a soldering iron. As her interest in the mechanical had turned into the way that signals could be sent and received to identify locations, the possibilities that could be achieved with such information had set her brain alight with wonder and excitement. The thrill of having an idea and of making it—

'What was wrong with it?'

Loukis's question cut through her thoughts, drawing her attention back to the present, back to him.

'The father wants to know, in case it happens again.'

'The compass needed to be recalibrated. It's a fairly common problem for that particular brand. He can look it up easily enough.'

It was only when she looked up at Loukis that she realised her mistake. Because how on earth would she explain how she had known that? His eyes didn't leave hers as he translated what she had said to the father. They didn't leave hers as the father proclaimed effusive thanks, tried to pay for their coffees—an offer that was dismissed by Loukis with a wave of his hand—and ran off after his happy son. No, it was Célia that broke the connection, unable to bear the scrutiny.

Over the past five years, only Ella had known about her drastic career change. She had been the only person to stick with her after her life had changed. Faces and so-called friends ran through her mind from that time 'before'. Hopes and dreams of trying to be seen by her father, be considered valuable, or even worthy in his eyes. But then he had taken her plans for agricultural drone technology for use in drought-affected areas of Africa and warped it, changed her good intentions in the most horrible way. Took them from her and used them for his true love: his own company.

She had spent the summer interning and impressing the research and development department in Paquet Industries as a way to try to be closer to her father. To impress him somehow. She'd inherited her father's genius, they'd all said. At the time she'd been pleased, so, so pleased. Only Ella had grumbled about being a genius in her own right. But Célia hadn't cared. Finally pleasing her father had been her only focus. Until someone had seen the technical specs she'd been working on as part of her degree over lunch one day. Closer and closer they had looked and once they'd realised what she'd done, they'd whisked her up to see her father. Her drawings, her ideas, had been pored over and over. At first by the manager, then by her father, then by other advisers and ultimately by lawyers.

God, she'd been so naïve. At first she'd been thrilled, excited, hopeful even. But then suddenly everything went quiet. People stopped talking about the project, behaving as if it had never happened. Her father became too busy to see her, to answer her calls even.

She'd wondered if perhaps they'd found something wrong with her designs and that had scoured her insides, devastating her in what she'd hoped to be 'the final' way, the 'only' way her father might find use or value, or even love. Three weeks after the internship had finished and she had returned to university, returned to Ella, who had comforted Célia in her bewilderment, she discovered what had happened. In the newspaper. The article had revealed a major deal between her father's company, Paquet Industries, and one of France's leading firearms manufacturers, proclaiming the revolutionising of drone technology as its key motivation.

What she was working on—designs to help agriculture in drought-affected areas, to allow better crop production, rapid identification of pest and fungal infestations, information on irrigation and so much more—had been used instead for murder. Justifications like *war on terror* and *border defence* and the little-known discipline of Measurement and Signature Intelligence had done nothing to assuage her guilt.

That her designs, her hopes and dreams had been so vilely abused had shocked her to her very core. Only Ella knew of the devastating guilt that had torn through Célia. That had seen her nearly drop out of college altogether. That had given her nightmares for months and months.

Her father had simply refused to speak of it, as if pretending it hadn't happened. Her mother had stood by him and, in Célia's mind, chosen his side. She hadn't spoken to her father in five years, her mother in three. And it still ached and twisted in her chest.

'Célia?'

Once again she had become so lost in her thoughts she had missed what Loukis had said. She brushed the hair that had fallen in front of her eyes aside, noticing how the green sapphires glinted in the sunlight, bringing her back to reality with a bump.

'Are you okay?' Loukis asked, a frown marring the near perfect features looking up at her.

'Yes. Sorry, what were you saying?'

'That we probably need to leave if we're going to make lunch.'

'Lunch?'

'Yes, you have an appointment.'

'An appointment?'

He nodded. 'One that would probably benefit from something more than you repeating my every word.'

Loukis stood from the table, but Célia remained on the chair.

'Is this a kind of sit-in?' he demanded, half amused.

'Yes. Until you tell me what's going on I'm not moving.'

'You sound like a child,' he said, now openly smiling, enjoying the slightly petulant bent to her tone. It had been much better than the series of emotions that he'd seen play upon her features after she had fixed the drone. Something that he had not forgotten and would most definitely be exploring at a later date. It was just that it didn't seem to fit. Not with Célia and who she was. And that made him uncomfortable. But he didn't have time right now for that.

'Lunch is where you are going to meet your next client,' he stated.

A look of horror passed over her features, new and different from before. 'But I'm not prepared. I don't know who they are or…anything. *Loukis.*' She used his name as both a question and punctuation. It was adorable.

'You are perfectly well prepared. You know your company inside out, you've got plenty of examples to draw from to illustrate any kind of point you need to make. And your soon-to-be new client has a low tolerance for unnecessary pomp, and a great deal of respect for straight talking. The two of you will get on wonderfully.'

Loukis gestured for Célia to go ahead before him, following behind a black-suited head waiter towards the table where Yalena Adeyemi and her husband sat, laughing quietly at something secret.

The moment Yalena caught sight of them, she stood from the table and greeted them both with a wide smile and excitement glinting in her espresso rich gaze.

'Loukis. It's been far too long,' she gently reprimanded. 'I'd be horrified that business has brought you finally back to socialising, if I wasn't so curious about the opportunity you've presented.' Without missing a beat, she turned to Célia. 'It's lovely to meet you, and *not* just because you're the "business opportunity",' Yalena said with genuine happiness.

Célia, who had been silent since he'd told her of their intended destination, came to life as if a switch had been flipped.

'Likewise. If I'm honest, I'm trying hard not to fan-girl at the moment. Your company has such a fantastic reputation and has achieved some really incredible things.'

Célia hadn't lied at all. She'd known of Yalena Adeyemi by reputation. As founder and CEO of one of the quickest growing peer-to-peer lending platforms, Yalena had been an inspiration for both Célia and Ella when starting up their own company.

'As does yours. Chariton Enterprises is steadily gaining quite a bit of notoriety, and,' she said, clearly noticing Célia's glance towards Loukis, 'not because of your recent exciting news. May I offer my congratulations on your engagement?'

Yalena gestured for them to sit, and Loukis made the introductions between Iannis, Yalena's husband, and Célia. Drinks were ordered, and small talk was made until they arrived.

'Iannis, why don't we leave the ladies to their business and go to the bar and gossip like the old miserable men that we are?' Loukis announced. Giving his wife a kiss on the cheek, Iannis followed Loukis away from the table and towards the bar as promised.

Célia was thankful for it. For some reason having Loukis there had put her on the back foot. As if embarrassed or worried about what he might think if he saw her in client mode. Which was doubly strange because he was a client himself.

She looked across at Yalena. Her close-cropped hair highlighted incredible cheekbones, gorgeous wide eyes and a ready smile. But for all of that, Célia knew that her mind was razor-sharp and her focus fierce.

'I was not just paying lip service, Célia. I am impressed with what you've done with your company, especially such a young one.'

'Thank you. It means a great deal to Ella, my business partner, and myself.'

She nodded. 'May I ask why?'

'Of course.'

Over the next hour Célia and Yalena discussed everything from why they had started their own businesses, what they had wanted from them and where they would like to go in the future. Each had been struck by how closely their motivations and desires had aligned and celebrated the successes and understood the challenges faced by the other. They were both in the business of matching like-minded clients, for their mutual benefit, and had faced many similar obstacles. This might have been why Yalena had probed deeper and more thoughtfully than most of Chariton's existing clients and, instead of dismissing outright the charity areas that Célia believed were the best fit for her peer-to-peer company, allowed her to explain her reasoning and interacted happily with Célia's initial thoughts on what kind of events would benefit them.

Yalena leaned back in her chair, her hands sweeping circles on the smooth white cloth.

'I know that look,' Loukis said from behind Célia's shoulder.

Yalena's thoughtful gaze turned into an amused scowl. 'You're ruining the moment.'

'No, I brought more champagne to celebrate.' The confidence in his voice sparking the thrill of excitement and a burst of hope in Célia.

'Does that mean I should have the contracts drawn up?' asked Célia with a smile.

'Yes. Most definitely yes. But that is all the business talk done for the day. Now. I want to hear *all* about the proposal!'

The lunch had lasted long into the afternoon and dusk was beginning to fall as Loukis paid the bill, much to Yalena's mocking disgruntlement. With deft acuity, he'd been able to keep much of the focus on Iannis and Yalena rather than on Célia and himself, Yalena's husband more than happy to indulge in schoolboy memories shared by them both. And Loukis realised that he'd missed it. Missed the easy laughter of un-weighted adult conversation. Much of the last three years of his life had been spent focused solely on Annabelle and shielding her from an outside gaze. Once Célia had realised that she'd secured not only another client, but one that had clearly inspired her, she had relaxed, joining in the gentle mockery between the two couples.

She had opened up under the gentle encouragement of those around her and it had been glorious. But he hadn't missed how she skirted around her own past, her parents and life before Chariton Enterprises. There had been a few of her own childhood stories of a Swiss boarding school with Ella, and her friend's marriage and recent baby news, but of herself, very little. And he still couldn't quite work out how the drone fitted with the charitable endeavours.

Emerging onto the stone street from the restaurant, they were greeted by a swarm of paparazzi and a hail of flashbulbs.

Yalena reached for him, kissing his cheeks in farewell.

'They're a little feisty this evening. Perhaps they caught wind of your news?' she said, sotto voce, to Célia and Loukis.

Célia looked towards him as if expecting an explanation, but he simply shrugged. 'It wasn't me.'

Iannis gave him a half-hug, ordered him not to let it go so long next time, turned to his wife and asked, 'Ready to run the gauntlet?'

The two disappeared and Loukis was a little

disconcerted that they didn't manage to take any of the vultures with them.

He placed an arm around Célia's shoulder. 'The car should be waiting in the back street. Ready?'

She tucked herself a little more deeply into his side. He knew it was for protection, but he couldn't help the streak of sensation that fired up and down the length of his body.

The moment they stepped forward, the questions began. The shouts and flashes were enough to bring on PTSD. He felt Célia tremble beside him and realised how intimidating and scary this would be for someone not accustomed to it.

'Congratulations! How did he do it, Célia?'

'Did he get down on one knee?'

'Ms d'Argent—any comment on the news about your father?'

Célia stumbled, her foot twisting, and she would have fallen had it not been for his arm around her shoulders. Loukis bit back a curse.

'What does François Paquet think of his future son-in-law?'

The name of the renowned French defence contractor cut through his anger with shocking intensity. Paquet was her father?

'Any response to the claims you've bagged another billionaire, Célia?'

'When was the last time you spoke to your ex, Marc Moreau?'

At this, he'd had enough. He turned to the seething mass around him. 'Ladies and gentlemen—' though the friendly appellation stuck in his throat '—is it not a bit uncouth to ask about the father, ex-partner and current fiancé all in the same breath?'

His tone had been light and mocking, received with laughter by most. But those that knew him, were familiar with him, held a trace of unease. For that was when he was at his most deadly.

'I would love to expound on this further, but as we have already agreed to a private interview with a *reputable* journalist, you will have to read it alongside everyone else.'

'We have an interview?' she whispered, from where she remained tucked into his shoulder as they rounded the corner towards the safe haven of the limousine.

'We will once you tell me what the hell all this is about,' he bit out. 'Get in the car.'

Célia slid into the limousine, her body protected from the strobe lights of the paparazzi, but her thoughts flayed by the repeated bursts of shocking white.

Her heart pounded in her chest. The rush of adrenaline soured by self-recrimination. She should have known that they would find out.

Should have prepared for it. Denial had not been enough to protect her from their piercing gaze.

The moment the door closed behind Loukis the sleek town car sped off, sending the sprawling mass scattering. The atmosphere in the dark interior was full of tension, as Loukis's barely leashed control seemed to strain against his hold over it. Her own pulse seemed to thump within the thick air.

'I...'

A gesture of his hand cut through the space between them, silencing her. She stifled back the words, unsure really where she would have begun anyway.

As the car wound its way towards Loukis's estate, the silence and tension filled the space between them to the point where Célia feared she might not be able to draw breath.

'Loukis—'

'François Paquet is your father?' he demanded.

All Célia could do was nod.

'And you—who demanded truth from me—didn't think to tell me?'

'He is no longer part of my life,' she insisted, as if she could make it true.

'Do you know what this fresh wave of interest from the press will do? They'll be frothing at the bit now. It will be impossible to keep the custody battle a secret, it will be impossible to...'

He trailed off. She knew he was thinking of how hard it would be to shield his sister from their penetrating gaze.

'*Christos*, Célia, if I'd known we could have come out in front of it, but now we're behind and…' His fury seemed to be working against his usual smooth calm, stopping words before he could form them. 'Why the hell didn't you tell me?'

'I haven't spoken to my father in five years. Not since I changed my degree, my name and left behind almost everything that connected me to that life.'

And with that she had lost any sense of family or belonging. As if she hadn't even realised until this moment just how isolated and lonely she felt, a sob rose in her chest that she desperately tried to stifle.

'Why? What happened?' He demanded explanations as if he could draw blood from a stone.

'I don't want to talk about it.'

'Tough,' he said mutinously. 'Because now I'm going to need to know everything. Including whoever the hell Marc Moreau is.'

The thought of what he wanted turned in Célia's stomach as they negotiated the bends in the road before pulling up to the estate. She watched him leave the car and stalk towards the front door of his home, realising that it was the first

time that Loukis had not opened the car door
for her. She was being punished, she realised.
Or, he was so consumed by the shocking revelation that he had simply forgotten it. Either way
it hurt, strangely.

Her feet felt heavy as she followed through the
open doorway, closing it behind her and wishing she could just as effectively close down the
events of that evening. She had been so happy!
She had been so excited when she'd known she
was having lunch with Yalena Adeyemi, and
when she'd realised that they'd get a chance to
work together? She'd been ecstatic. She should
have known better. Because the last time she'd
felt that excited, that thrilled, as if on the brink of
something marvellous, everything had turned to
ash. And once again, it was because of her father.

CHAPTER EIGHT

SHE FOUND LOUKIS pacing the living-room area with a drink already in his hand, his hair ruffled as if he'd run his hand through it several times before she'd entered the room.

'Sit,' he commanded.

'I'll stand, thank you,' she said, unconsciously echoing the last time they'd had an uncomfortable conversation in this room. It was, she realised, an act of self-preservation. As if her subconscious knew that flight would be easier from standing rather than from sitting on the plush soft sofa.

He looked at her as if to indicate that he had not *asked*, but she remained where she stood. Because now she was angry. How dared he find fault with a reputation not of her own making, when his was so debauched? She needed to cling to that anger, because beneath it was a layer of hurt and betrayal so deeply entrenched, she was terrified of hauling it out for inspection. But even that, she realised, covered a guilt that had motivated every single decision she'd made in the last five years. And no matter what, she knew she'd never reveal that to Loukis.

'Start with your father.'

'My father took something of mine and used it for his own purposes.'

He looked at her as if to say, 'Is that all?' and she wanted to scream.

'What, he withheld your pocket money?'

'Don't be crass,' she replied, this time very consciously echoing his own words once fired at her down the phone.

'What, then?' he demanded, his patience clearly wearing thin.

'He took my technical specs for a more efficient drone tracking system.'

The look on his face might have been comical had it not been so painful.

'What?'

She'd known he'd have trouble either understanding her or believing her, either way he clearly needed more of an explanation.

'Five years ago I was studying a graduate degree at the ENS in Sciences, specialising in mathematics and computer sciences. Please don't look at me as if I've just sprouted a second head. It's…patronising and infuriating.'

'I'm not being patronising,' he said defensively. 'I have clearly only known you as a successful humanities entrepreneur. The computer science thing doesn't seem to fit.'

'I happened to be very good at *"the computer science thing"*, thank you.'

'Which begs the question,' he replied, as if she had only proved his point.

'As a child, it became quite clear that I had an affinity with computers and technology. To me, they always made sense. There was clarity in ones and zeros, an unwavering logic. I liked the challenge they presented and revelled in working around and within them to get what I wanted. As part of my degree at ENS, I knew that I would have to find an internship to support my education and thought that Paquet Industries would be perfect.' She had told herself that then, and told Loukis the same lie now. But, really, it had been more than that—she just didn't want to open that painful truth to herself, or Loukis.

'I had been using their workshops to work on my dissertation project. One of the senior managers had seen what I was working on and the next thing I knew it was taken from me. Used in a...used in a very different way from what I had intended.' She felt the familiar rush of anger, the ache of her father refusing to speak to her.

'Because you had signed an intellectual property waiver for work done while interning.'

Surprised, she looked up at Loukis, immediately appreciating the quick mind that had made his own company such a shocking international success.

'Yes.'

'I get how that must have been frustrating, but, what? This is about money? Recognition for your designs?'

'No, it's not that!' She knew that was how it would have been seen had the news got out with no acknowledgement of the wracking guilt she still faced to this day. She couldn't, wouldn't share with Loukis what her plans had been used for, horrified by the sheer thought of his reaction, but she could try to make him realise why, could try to make him understand.

'I…growing up with my father wasn't…' She took a deep breath. This was so much harder than she'd thought it would be. 'He was a difficult man. Exacting, focused…'

'Demanding?' Loukis prompted.

'No, actually. He wasn't. Because he never really expected anything of me other than to be seen and not heard. He'd always wanted a son to pass on Paquet Industries to, but after me, my mother was unable to fall pregnant again. So, in a way, I became a representation of his failure, I think. I can only guess, because he hardly credited me with such an honest explanation or outpouring.

'And in my childlike logic, I thought that if I could prove myself of use, if I could harness my skills for my father's company he might… He might finally see me as worthy.' She shrugged as if her innocent conclusion didn't hold such a world of pain within it.

'And Marc Moreau? Who is he?'

'He works for the Ministère de la Jeunesse et des Sports,' Célia said, trying not to flinch at Loukis's tone.

'The Ministry of Sport?'

'And youth affairs, yes.'

Loukis frowned, as displeased. 'Okay. Let's try this again. Who is he to you?'

'My ex-fiancé.'

'I gathered that much, Célia.'

She inhaled the tense air between them, trying to fortify herself. 'I met Marc at boarding school. He joined when we were sixteen and was…charming and playful. Fun. He could have had his pick of any of the female students, but he was only interested in me,' she concluded with a shrug. 'I was surprised, but flattered. I enjoyed his attention.' It had been a gift even then, before she'd realised just how distant her father was and how desperate it had made her for affection. 'He ended up at the same university as me and Ella.

He'd wanted me to move into an apartment with him, but Ella and I had always talked about living together so I said no. But we went out, restaurants, clubs, parties. I didn't really enjoy it—' she could see that now '—my course required a lot of work, but he always seemed so disappointed when I would say no. Only after did I realise that the restaurants were always booked in my name, the VIP sections in clubs, the party invitations.' And she felt like such a fool.

'Over the four years we'd been together, he'd spent quite a bit of time with my family. He seemed to get on with my father, more than I did at least. He made a monumental effort with him. And I thought it was for me. Until I broke ties with my father. Until I changed my name. And somehow in his eyes, that made me a changed person. He refused to understand why what my father had done was wrong. Insisted that I try to make it up with him.

'When I refused, he began to retreat. Telling me I'd changed, telling me that I wasn't fun any more. He made me doubt myself, and it hurt to force myself to be with him, to keep a smile on my face I didn't feel surrounded by people I didn't know. Because I didn't want to lose him too.' She felt the ache building in her chest. Hating to admit such a thing, feeling so very vulnerable to tell Loukis this. But she knew that he deserved what little she could tell him. 'Slowly, bit by bit he removed himself from my life. I didn't notice at first, but then it would be days, or a week that I wouldn't see or hear from him. Ella convinced me to have it out with him, if anything just to let him know how I felt.

'It was awful. He said it was all my fault. The time and energy he'd put into me wasted. How he didn't want a *girlfriend*—you see, I'd been relegated by that point—who couldn't…*give* him anything. What use was I if I was not perfect?'

In that instant, she realised the truth of the past. As if saying it out loud had somehow conjured the shocking revelation that she had never been wanted. Not for herself. Only for what she could do and be for someone. She had been used by her father, by Marc…and each time she had failed to live up to their expectations, had failed to be what they wanted and in that moment she felt that she had never felt truly loved.

Loukis pressed a drink into her hands and she realised she was shaking.

'And I demanded the same,' Loukis said softly into the silence.

'*Non,*' she replied, shaking her head. 'I knew what you expected from the beginning. You didn't…'

'Lie?' he said, letting loose a curse that surprised her.

* * *

Loukis let out the burst of air locked in his lungs, trying to marry the two vastly different aspects of her personality—the technical expert and the head of a humanities charity—and make them somehow fit with the guilt stirring in his veins. Guilt because, no matter how much she might try to absolve him, he had taunted her with perfection. With the need to be everything that her father and ex-fiancé had unfathomably found wanting in her. Guilt because, even as he knew how much it cost her, he still needed that perfection. For Annabelle. And that scoured his veins and struck his heart. Because it was a hurt that called to him. A hurt that he recognised so painfully as a mirror reflection, in some ways, of his own.

His father had never disapproved of him, nor his mother—they had both been so preoccupied with each other, he had barely even been a consideration. Oh, his father had tried after the divorce, but he'd never been the same, just a shell of the man he once had been.

But he did know how that affected him. It had seen him spiral into a level of selfishness that had him desperate to indulge in every whim, every pleasure, everything he felt had been denied him in his childhood. Looking back now, he could see the mask that had hidden that childhood hurt. The rakish playboy, the careless façade had created a barrier between him and the world…him and hurt.

But all the while he had been indulging, had been consumed by satisfying his wants and needs with a selfishness that shamed him now, Célia had chosen a different path to direct her energies. He wanted her to see that. Wanted to help her realise that she was so much more. So worthy of more than whatever pittance her father had meted out.

'You know that what you've achieved since then is incredible.' It was a statement. A reassurance. 'You did it without the backing of a name and an existing company, which is far more than I've ever done.'

She turned aside, as if not even wanting to accept the compliment.

'Célia, look at me,' he commanded, bringing her face round to his with the crook of his finger at her chin. He took in her large, molten amber eyes, the same fiery colour shining from her hair. The pale, creamy skin blushed by a tint of peach, sweet enough to want to…

He stifled the wicked sensual pull he felt, the desperate urge to taste more than the simple starter he had experienced the night before, to delve into everything she had to offer. None of which he could do, or even entertain the thought of. Bringing anything more into the precarious agreement they had could bring the whole thing crashing down about them. As if torn between reluctance and the desire to touch, he reached his arm out around her shoulders and drew her to him, the action soothing something within them both.

'I mean it. You should be incredibly proud of what you've achieved. Yalena—'

'Was only interested in me because of you,' she interrupted.

'Yalena,' he pressed on, 'wouldn't have agreed to partner with you had it not been because you are worthy of it. She's a great friend, but she wouldn't even do that for me. You are the head of a company that has seen great success in the first three years because of the drive and determination you have brought to it and that should not be dismissed. You have a power that it pains me to see you don't realise. And no one, not your father, nor some stupid ex who didn't realise what he had before throwing it away, nor *I* can take that away. Only you can do that to yourself. And until you cast that aside, you won't realise just how much more you can achieve.'

As Célia felt the words settle about her, she began to feel it. The power that he had talked of, the pride that he had shown her through his eyes. It soothed, and it helped. But she couldn't deny that she still felt...still felt that she wanted more. More from Loukis.

'What happens now?' she asked, her voice still a little shaky from emotion.

'Now? Now I need to know how quickly you can plan an engagement party.'

Célia had laughed at the idea that an engagement party would distract the press enough from her notorious father's identity. But the moment it was announced, they had behaved exactly how Loukis had promised they would.

Célia felt a fresh wave of goosebumps crest across her skin. Not from the fresh sea-salt-laden air, but the nervousness for what was to come. Standing on the deck of the most luxurious yacht she'd ever seen, she couldn't quite believe that all of this was for her. *For them.*

The first guests were due to arrive any moment now and she felt poised on the brink of something she couldn't put a name to. In the last week, since the night of the press furore, things had been...easier between her and Loukis. She had feared that sharing a bit of her past would disappoint him, or disgust him. But it had been freeing. A weight had lifted. Not all, but some of it. She had taken his words that night to heart. Allowed them to settle around her and drawn strength from them.

She refused to turn for the sound of Loukis's footsteps making their way towards where she stood at the balcony of the yacht, looking out over the port of Piraeus. The sun was hovering halfway between the zenith and the horizon, bright and still powerful even at this time in the afternoon.

She was amazed that she didn't flinch when she felt Loukis draw the silk scarf that had fallen into the crook of her arm upwards over her shoulder. All these little touches, the sheer proximity of him, sent a thrill through her, as if the power of them had built over the last few days. Something she had come to long for, as if the dizzying rush of adrenaline and desire had become addictive to her, and she just about managed to stop herself from leaning into him.

She did flinch, however, when he drew her to his side, just as she'd wanted him to. Not because of him, no. She flinched as the electric starburst cascaded through her the moment the bare skin at her side met his forearm.

Never before would she have dared to wear such a thing. But she had been unable to resist. The night of their conversation about her father, Loukis had made her realise how much she had buried in the last five years. It wasn't just her relationship with her parents, but with herself. Her sense of self. And she wanted that back. Wanted to be the powerful, glorious woman Loukis told her he saw. So she had chosen the most daring of designs and colours. The rich Prussian blue of the material suited her and the high-waisted long maxi skirt was a dream, unfurling from her in smooth, silky waves every time she moved. But the cropped top that clung to her curves and an area of her stomach she wasn't sure had seen the light of day for years had given her pause. Until she'd caught the way that Loukis had looked at her. Was, in fact, looking at her now.

That alone sent a shocking thrill to her very core.

'Annabelle is set up for an evening of junk food and films,' he said, turning to look out on the horizon, breaking whatever sensual hold he had on her.

'Did you tell her I said hi?' she asked after she had navigated the sudden shift between them.

'She's rather attached to her new nickname.' Célia smiled.

'Leya's parents will bring her over to the island on the boat tomorrow and Tara will arrive just before the custody hearing.'

Célia was curious about this island estate Loukis had told her they'd be going to after the party. Thankful that they'd finally be escaping the narrow-focused lens of the paparazzi after what felt like weeks of fighting headlines and photo opportunities, she heaved a sigh of relief tinged with excitement. And was also surprised to be looking forward to seeing Annabelle again. All of this had been with her shadow in the background. And once Loukis had seemed to take on board what she'd said about Meredith and his true motivations, he hadn't relaxed, exactly, but had been refocused in a way. More determined to ensure Annabelle's happiness. To a woman who had been so badly betrayed by her own father, it had touched her. Warmed her to Loukis, even when he was being his most autocratic.

But her thoughts went back to the island that was somewhere out there in the sea before her. He had told her about it, about the private beach, about a bit of the architecture…but he hadn't said anything about the bedrooms. About *his* room. And suddenly she couldn't shake the thought of it. Of sharing a bed with him. Of exploring where those touches might lead. This evening, tonight, she'd be sharing a room with her fiancé.

She wasn't sure if Loukis was aware of the way his fingers traced the bare skin at her side. He certainly couldn't know the chaotic thoughts it sent through her mind, the wants it sent through her body.

The sounds of a car door closing cut through the background noise of the port, and they turned in unison to see Ella and Roman making their way down the red-carpeted gangplank with something a little like awe on Ella's face, and easy acceptance on Roman's dark features.

Célia couldn't tell if it was Ella or herself that had let out the little squeal of delight when they finally saw each other, both rushing forwards for a hug.

From the corner of her eye, Célia saw the two men greet each other in the half-hug and back slap that had become internationally recognisable as the greeting of men.

For a moment, her breath caught in her lungs. Both men looked as if they'd just stepped out of a fashion shoot. Impossibly tall, painfully handsome, Roman dressed in a dark linen suit and Loukis in one of a blue that echoed her own clothing's colour, they were a sight to behold.

'Loukis,' Ella called across the deck. 'You may have her for the rest of your life, but for this evening, she is *mine*,' she mock taunted, with absolutely no idea of the effect her words had on Célia.

Her gaze flew immediately to Loukis, who seemed in an instant to understand exactly what had caused a streak of lightning to burst through her in shock. All these weeks, everything they'd done had been to promote their fake engagement. But the people gathering this evening, friends and family and others…they expected a wedding. They believed in a future that Célia would never have. A love.

* * *

Ella had whisked Célia off and then more guests
had arrived, slowly filling the beautiful wooden
deck, so much so that he only seemed to catch
glimpses of his beautiful fiancée through tai-
lored suits and exquisite dresses. The jewellery
on display could have made the stars jealous, as
if every person there had known that they might
appear in the next day's newspapers.

The interview with *Hello!* Greece had been a
six-page spread with posed portraits in a rented
apartment overlooking the Acropolis. He ensured
that the focus was not on Célia's father, but about
what she had achieved, how she had wanted to
do it herself without her father's influence. The
piece was positive and glowing and not because
of him, but the genuine interest and excitement
from the journalist. Since the article had come
out more than twelve international business fig-
ures had contacted Chariton, causing Célia to
remark that he had given her a bonus. The way
she made it sound, as if his part of the 'deal'
was done, had unaccountably caused a sense of
dismay within him, resentment—he reluctantly
admitted—at the reminder of their agreement.

He caught another glimpse of her, with Yalena
and Ella, the three women laughing together and
it was a sight to behold. The moment he'd seen
Célia he'd almost asked her to change. She was

stunning in a way that made him want to keep her to himself. To hide her beauty, hoard it all for him. But saying that would reveal too much. Reveal just how much he was affected by the sensual torment he had ignited the first time he had touched her in the restaurant.

By the bar he saw Iannis and Roman and was just about to join them when another car drew up to the yacht's gangplank. They had been due to set sail at any moment, so he turned to greet the latecomers, ready—along with the staff—to hurry them onto the deck before the departure when he stopped midstride, shock and fury turning him rigid.

He purposefully released the clench in his jaw, aware that any slight reaction would draw the gazes of the guests. He could almost feel the shutters on cameras clicking through a hundred photos as if the press had expected this moment, wanted it even.

Meredith walked onto the deck of the yacht like a queen ready to receive her due. In her wake followed a large, round, red-cheeked man improbably wearing a Stetson, grinning as if he was genuinely in ignorance of the horror show this was about to descend into.

Loukis couldn't let that happen. He didn't know what game Meredith was playing, he certainly knew that she hadn't been on the invite list, but he could hardly kick her off the boat, much as he wanted to, as the gangplank was rolled away and the ship's captain sounded the horn to announce their departure from the dock.

His mother's gaze found his and for a moment, just the barest of seconds, he couldn't quite decipher the look that crossed her features, before it was schooled in that same plastic fakery he was used to seeing splashed across the headlines that had decried her infidelity all those years ago.

She made straight for him. Unsurprising, since she had never seemed to shy from a fight with his father.

'Darling,' she called to him, drawing a few curious glances from those about him who knew about their precarious relationship. She placed a red-taloned finger on his forearm and leaned in for air kisses two inches from either cheek.

'What are you doing here?' he growled, keeping his voice low so that only she could hear.

'I came to wish my son all the happiness in the world for his engagement,' she said loudly enough for others to hear and in a tone that completely ignored the hostility rising from him in waves. 'Let me introduce Byron Fairchild.'

'Nice to meetcha,' he said, his Texan drawl so strong the last two words rolled into one and sounded vaguely like a south American cocktail.

He felt the man's beefy hand encase his, and

Loukis searched the man's features for something other than genuine delight. Had Meredith not told him anything? 'What a gal you've got here,' he said, casting his gaze around the deck, clearly speaking of the yacht, rather than Célia, who Loukis suddenly wanted to protect, to hide from his mother's piercing gaze as she, too, searched the boat with an equally assessing gaze.

'As is our Annabelle. She's such a sweetheart,' Byron said without awareness of how his use of our cut through Loukis like a knife.

Loukis felt a lurch in his stomach, from the propulsion of the yacht's engine or the reaction to his mother's presence, he couldn't tell. It had been three years since Meredith had deposited his sister on his doorstep. And before that? Fifteen years since the night she'd promised to come back for him, promised to take him with her. But then he'd heard the argument between his parents. Heard his father offer to pay her an obscene amount to leave Loukis with him. He'd been so sure she would refuse. So sure that she would be outraged and furious. But she'd agreed. And Loukis had never seen her again.

'It's been too long, darling.'

Not long enough had been on the tip of his tongue, when he felt an arm at his back, lending him strength and levelling him in the moment. Had she somehow sensed that he would need this?

'Hello,' Célia said, reaching out her free hand to greet Meredith, whose practised smile turned positively feline.

'So you are the one who has tamed the notorious playboy.'

It was a phrase he knew that Célia had both heard and read many times, but to hear it from his mother, it cut him deep. Célia was so much more than that.

'Célia d'Argent, Meredith…forgive me, I don't know which name you're going under these days. It wouldn't still be Liordis,' he said, the bitter humour lacing his tone enough to make both women momentarily pause. 'And you never much seemed to care for your maiden name. Are you back to being Meredith Leda, or—'

'Timone,' she interrupted, clearly not caring for his words. 'I'm going by Timone.'

'But soon to be Fairchild, yeah?' the brash Texan said, shouldering Meredith in a way that she must have been braced for otherwise she would have been sent flying. Loukis happily caught the flare of frustration before Meredith schooled her features and hooked her arm around her fiancé's.

'Just think, the two of us, engaged and on the brink of such happiness,' Meredith said, not looking so much at Byron, but between Célia and Loukis.

He genuinely couldn't tell whether her engagement with Fairchild was as fake as his own, but whether Byron himself knew that or not was another matter. As the large man engaged Célia in a conversation, he finally turned to take in his mother.

Her hair was still the same brilliant blonde he remembered from his childhood—whether by artifice or nature, he couldn't tell. Faint lines around her eyes had escaped the pull of Botox he was sure had been used liberally across features that felt so devastatingly familiar. Seeing her in person was so much more…affecting than on the front page.

'Meredith—'

'Where is Annabelle?' she asked, looking around as if she might be there.

'Not here,' he replied, viciously enjoying the look of frustration on her features. 'Why are you?' he demanded again.

'I wanted to talk to you about dropping the custody case.'

He scoffed. Loud and low and he could have sworn he saw her flinch, but instead he believed the avarice he saw glinting in her eyes.

'How much?'

'How much what?' she asked, her artificial

confusion grating against the frayed edge of his nerves.

'How much would it take to walk away? Five million. Ten?' His tone spoke of boredom, all the while his pulse raged in his chest as she finally revealed her true intentions. He knew that this would be the way he could finally get rid of her. Because he would pay. He would pay whatever price she—

'I don't want your money, Loukis.'

'You don't need to play this game with me, Meredith. I know how this works, remember? I've been here before. What was it again? Twenty million for the divorce, and an extra ten if you left me behind?'

'Is that what this is about? You want to punish me?'

'No.' Although his inner voice cried liar. Loukis kept his voice low and his words lethal. 'I will not allow you to hurt Annabelle. I will do whatever it takes to ensure that she stays with me, safely and happily, because I love her and want the best for her.'

'Then you will understand that I will do the same. Because I do love her, Loukis.'

You just don't love me, he raged silently, cursing his own weakness.

She nodded to herself and turned, searching her fiancé out amongst the crowd from where

Célia had guided him, summoning him to her as if by some previously agreed signal.

'We'll be leaving now.'

'We're in the middle of the damn sea, Meredith. But I should not be surprised to find that you already had your escape route planned. Leaving is something you are clearly very good at.'

She resisted the barbed comment, and as she waited for Byron, she took in Célia as well. Loukis felt even more alert, poised, ready to defend what was his against his own mother.

'I'm pleased at least that you have her. The way you look at her...' Meredith trailed off. 'Was more than I ever looked at your father. But I do mean it. I want Annabelle with me and I'll do whatever it takes to get her back.'

And on that cryptic note, she drew Byron away towards the back of the yacht, where he could see a smaller speedboat had slunk through the barrage of press boats following in their wake, up behind the yacht, and was being frantically moored out of the way of the jet stream of the engine.

Célia looked up at him, the concern clear in her face, and he couldn't help himself. He needed it, he needed her. His lips crashed down on hers, shocking them both, each feeding off the adrenaline, drawing strength and more from the heady impact of the kiss.

CHAPTER NINE

DUSK HAD FALLEN, casting the sea about them in an inky darkness that was pierced by the bright lights strung overhead. The deck was still full of guests, though the staff weaving through them with silver trays of champagne and canapés had lessened in the last hour as Célia and Loukis's departure grew closer.

A boat was to meet them and ferry them to Loukis's island home while the yacht returned the guests back to the port at Piraeus. Célia drew the silk wrap around her shoulders to ward off the sea breeze, undeterred by the large heaters placed strategically across the deck. She wasn't sure what had passed between Loukis and his mother, but ever since they had left, her fiancé-for-now had been distant. Oh, he'd played his part well, smiled and laughed with the guests, pronouncing him the happiest man, the luckiest. But that kiss had been full of so much more than expediency or efficiency to communicate their 'engagement'. It had shocked her, the ferocity of need that whipped through her, that she felt from *him*. Had it not been for the wolf whistles that had cut the kiss short, she would have been lost. Lost to him and to whatever it was that he had called forth.

And since then, he'd remained just out of reach. Never staying long in the same circle she was, hovering some distance away, ready with some excuse to withdraw. Having become so accustomed to his touch, his presence, the feel of him at her side, Célia felt strangely adrift. As if she'd done something wrong. As if she was being punished, or denied something, without explanation or understanding. It had nestled into the space she kept reserved for her father and her ex. And she hated it.

Had he too realised what she had? That they had spent the entire evening lying to their friends, their loved ones? That the happiness of the guests had started to grate because they were celebrating something that was not to be? Célia's heart ached a little at the thought and she chastised herself for it.

One of the reasons she had been happy to agree to Loukis's demand was because she would know where she stood. That he would not demand anything more than appearance. That there were clear lines that neither would broach.

But she wouldn't lie to herself. Not now. She knew her body's reaction to Loukis. She knew that she had somehow come to want him more than anything she had ever experienced before. In the last few weeks she had understood, appreciated and even liked him more for his need to protect his sister. The kind of protection that had never been afforded to her. She wanted to know what that was like. To be able to rely upon a man so strong in his conviction, so powerful, so…enthralling.

She had come to want to be the woman he saw. The proud, accomplished, driven woman who was just as powerful as he. And as she tried that woman on for size she was surprised to find how intoxicating that sense of power was, how… hedonistic.

It was with painful irony that she realised this just as Loukis seemed intent on withdrawing from her and she now looked upon their retreat to his island estate with trepidation. She knew what she wanted…but would he give that to her? She was not naïve. She knew that she had seen the flame of arousal and need in him. Knew that he was affected as she had been, not just by the kiss earlier, but each touch and caress that drew them inexplicably towards a point of no return. But she could also sense the barrier between them. The one that held him on one side and her on the other—an immoveable wall that she wanted to tear down. But could she risk it? Could she give into her desires, but still protect her heart?

Her heart wasn't involved, she told herself sternly. It wasn't what Loukis wanted and it certainly wasn't part of the deal. The irony was that although he needed the perfect fiancée, it wasn't real…so perhaps she didn't need to be so perfect. And it was precisely that which gave her desires, her wants, free rein.

A smartly dressed man in a Captain's uniform appeared at her side, informing her that it was time. Célia knew he meant that the boat had arrived to whisk her and Loukis away from their guests, but she couldn't help but feel that it was also some internal battle cry. That it was time. For her finally to ask for what she wanted, to demand it from him.

The guests laughed as Ella gave Célia one last hug, shouting demands to Loukis to bring her friend back safely, as if they were going on a holiday or, worse, that he might actually keep her. For ever.

The words hung in Loukis's mind, taunting him. He shouldn't have done it. The kiss had been over three hours ago now and he could still taste her. Feel her lips beneath his, the spike in his adrenaline washing away the bitterness of his encounter with Meredith, consuming all his thoughts and focus on the sensual delight Célia offered. She had returned his kiss with a fervour that had both shocked and aroused. Until the wolf whistles of the guests on the yacht had cut through the moment of madness.

He hadn't touched her since. Not even in the little ways he had become accustomed to doing, in the name of…he had been a fool. Lying to himself. Those touches had nothing to do with her getting used to him and had been only about him laying a hand on her. Teasing himself, testing himself, trying to prove to himself that he wasn't the playboy any more. That he could resist temptation.

In the last three years he *had* resisted the temptation of many beautiful women. He was most definitely not the reckless playboy of his youth. The problem was *Célia*. Not him. She had called to him like a siren from the very beginning. Even now, as he waved goodbye to the guests from the speedboat moored beside the yacht, he remembered their first encounter. She had presented an unusual challenge and, despite the hideous *beigeness* of her T-shirt at the time, he had still seen the beauty she worked so hard to hide.

But the challenge had morphed in the last few weeks, until the bright point of its edge had cut through the sensual miasma between them and he'd realised that the real threat would be to act on his desire for her.

The way you look at her...

His mother's voice taunted him even as he did take his fill. The yacht's Captain had taken her arm and was helping her down into the speedboat beside him. He observed a brief glimpse of smooth pale skin between the high skirt and the cropped top she wore, the way her hips swayed as she took her first steps towards him and the smile across her features and a thrill in her eyes he wanted to turn away from. For it was not excitement at the boat ride towards his island home, but something else. A deeper, darker pull, tempting him. Taunting him.

But the risk was too great. Hadn't Meredith shown that tonight? Nothing could come between himself and his custody of Annabelle. Not even the woman coerced into helping him get that very thing.

As he pulled down on the throttle of the boat he was piloting himself, he relished the roar of the engines, hoping that in some way they would burn away the ferocious need that held him tight in its grip.

They had moored at a jetty after about forty minutes on the speedboat. The noise from the twin engines making any form of communication impossible. Not that Célia had tried. She might know her own body's desires, but she could also tell his. Loukis had built a wall between them ever since that kiss. One that she wanted to tear down.

It was as if a line had been drawn in the sand—one she would readily cross, yet he remained on the other side. But it was his fault. He had started this, he had drawn this impossible need from within her and now she was angry. Angry that he was seemingly walking away.

Once again, his automatic sense of chivalry had been lost as he forged ahead up the dark path, leaving her to follow in his wake. Célia had been shut out before, so many times that the feeling was painfully familiar. But she wouldn't have it. Not this time.

As Loukis opened the front door to a sprawling estate, she saw none of the beauty and opulence she had come to expect from Loukis. She saw nothing but his back as he walked further into the property she really couldn't care less for.

'Don't do this. Don't ignore me,' she called after him as he stalked through the dark rooms offering only shapes in the gloom to identify their use.

'The bedroom is upstairs. There's no one here, so you can—'

'Don't. Ignore. Me.' The words held a barely

leashed anger that had been brewing long before
she had met Loukis.

'What do you want from me?' he demanded,
spinning to turn on her. The moonlight glinting
through impossibly large windows picking out
the harsh lines of anger on his features.

'I want you to stop playing. I want you to stop
hiding.'

'Hiding?' he breathed out on a harsh laugh.
'You accuse *me* of hiding?'

'Yes. Right now, I am. Because you *are* hiding.'

He shook his head. 'Go to bed.'

'I'm not some child you can easily dismiss. I
will not be sent to bed.' Her breath caught before
she issued a demand of her own. 'Unless you are
in it with me.'

'No.'

'Really? You were the one who said—'

'I know what I said,' he interrupted as if not
wanting the reminder of his own demands. 'But
I was wrong.'

'That must have hurt.'

'What?'

'Admitting that you were wrong.'

'Don't be—'

'Crass?' It was Célia that interrupted this time.

'Naïve!' he countered with anger. 'Do you

think I can risk this? Meredith showing up to-night—'

'Has nothing to do with what is going on be-tween us. So. Next?'

'Next what?'

'Next excuse to avoid what is going on be-tween us.'

Loukis shook his head again, wondering how on earth Célia managed to oscillate between proud and determined and fearful and shy. He couldn't be here. He couldn't stand here and see her like this, because she was simply magnifi-cent. Demanding what she wanted, powerful and righteous. And it was the most devastatingly at-tractive thing he'd ever seen.

She was a siren. Calling to him, calling *for* him. But he just couldn't. The risk was too great.

'There is nothing going on between us, other than a fake engagement.'

'Liar.'

She stalked towards him, capturing his gaze as the silky material unfurled around her legs, as the sensual pull in her eyes demanded, ca-joled, taunted. She reached him, her head lifted towards his, the scent of her perfume soothing as much as enticing, the feel of her body's heat crashing against him more forcefully than the waves he'd battled to reach the island.

'Kiss me.'

He said nothing.

'Kiss me. Without the paparazzi watching. Without being on display. Show me, prove to me that there's nothing between us,' she demanded.

'I'm not playing this game.'

'This,' she said, reaching for his fiercely clenched jaw, 'is not a game any more.'

He didn't move. He couldn't. Because everything in him wanted to act, touch, taste. And there would be no turning back from that. So he stayed stock-still, as if made from marble. He had to.

She reached up on tiptoes and pressed a soft kiss against his lips. He resisted the gentle pressure at his neck from where she had reached, guiding him to her, deeper into her, hating that it must have felt like rejection to her, but unable to give in to her demand.

But a hint of the sweep of her tongue against his lips pierced his defences. Kiss after kiss, her mouth opening further in fractions that made him mad with need. The warm press of her breasts against his chest, her thighs against his within millimetres of where his hands had fisted by his sides.

And then, as if sensing his reluctance, she pulled away. And the look in her eyes crushed the air in his lungs. The raw yearning, need, and sadness in the large amber orbs was too much. His hands flew to her face, holding her, stopping her retreat and at the precise moment he should have walked away, he stepped forward, his mouth crashing down on hers and greedily taking everything she had to offer.

He breathed her in, his tongue demanding entrance, glorying in the feel of her beneath his lips and hands. He drew her to him as if he could consume her, as if he could steal something from her and keep it with him.

Need became a primal roar, echoing throughout his body, crying more, crying now. Only the soft moans Célia made cut through the raging pulse in his ears causing him to stop, to try and pull back the control he had lost so shockingly easily.

Their harsh breathing echoed between them. He saw the flash of her white teeth digging into a bottom lip he had just thoroughly ravished. It was too much. He wanted it for himself. And that was the problem. This wasn't about the custody battle, the press, or even his mother. He needed Célia for himself. And that was untenable.

'Is that what you wanted, Célia?' he demanded. 'To bring me to my knees? To make me beg?'

He made to turn away, the words bringing forth shocking images of exactly what he wanted to do to her, *for* her, but her hand reached for him before he could.

He had expected words, pleading, impassioned perhaps. But instead the silence remained as she lifted his hand and placed it high on her breast, covering her heart where he felt her pulse rage against his palm. A beat that echoed within him just as incessant, just as demanding, just as out of control.

'I am the one on my knees. I am the one begging,' she said resolutely.

'You should never have to beg, Célia. You are worth more than that.'

'I know my worth. I know yours. And I know what I want.'

The heat from her body beneath his hand wrapped around him, drawing him towards her, even as he fought every inch of it.

'I know what is at stake, Loukis. And I promise you, I would not jeopardise that. Ever.'

'This isn't about Annabelle, Célia. It's about you,' he said roughly. 'I am not capable of giving you what you deserve. Not now. Not ever.'

He had to say the words. Force them to his lips. It was the truth, the deepest truth he'd ever spoken to a woman. Célia deserved so much more than this. She deserved a future and he couldn't give her that.

'I understand.'

He had thought that would do it. That she would finally walk away, but instead, she placed her hand over his, where it still rested against her heart.

'And it doesn't change a thing.'

Célia's pulse sped under the heat of his palm secured by her own. She knew what she was saying, what she was asking him for. Neither of them were ready or willing for anything more than perhaps just this night. But she would not walk away from this easily. If, for even a second, she thought this heady, half-mad desire was one-sided, she never would have raised it. But she knew. She knew he felt what she did, wanted what she did. It was as if acknowledging, owning, the truth of their desire was the only thing that could save her from the precipice she was hurtling towards. As if he were the only thing that could save her from it.

He searched her gaze as if hunting for a flaw, a contradiction, a doubt in her mind. But there was none.

She became so aware of his hand on her chest, resting beneath her own, as if that one point of connection bound them together on the brink of action or inaction. Her body overly sensitised, wanting more, desperate for more. But he had to choose this. She couldn't force this on him no matter how much she felt he wanted it.

This time she turned away, feeling as if she had lost the battle. Until his fingers wrapped around her arm, drawing her back to him in a kiss that obliterated the memories of all other kisses.

She opened her mouth to the pressure of his lips, his tongue, let him angle her head to where he wanted it, because it was so impossibly good. Everything in her rose to cry *yes*. This was what she had wanted. Loukis, unfettered, let loose amongst the pleasure they were seeking.

As his hands released their hold and travelled across her body, Célia revelled in the heat of them through the material, and then, when they reached the expanse of uncovered skin at her waist, his fingers hooking at her hip and pulling her against him roughly.

Gone was civility, gone was propriety, gone were the rules that had both bound them together and kept them apart. Every touch, every kiss made her feel worshipped. As if he were gaining as much from her own pleasure as she was.

It was a feeling she had never experienced before. The riotous cascade of sensation, desire, was hedonistic. Beneath her palms his chest was firm, as she fisted his shirt in her hands and drew him closer. It wasn't enough. She feared, silently, that it might never be enough.

He stepped back, pulling her with him, until he came up against the wall, imprisoning himself within her embrace. He reached for her knee beneath the silky folds of the skirt, hooking it over his hip and bringing her core against the hard ridge of his arousal.

Instinctively she arched against his chest, her hands moving upwards to frame his face, exulting in the feeling of his palms against the skin on her shoulders and arms, the warmth and security she experienced as he wrapped an arm around her and held her to him. It was an anchor in the storm of emotions that threatened to wash her out to sea. Because she trusted him.

The thought took her by surprise, momentarily stopping her. Loukis pulled back, releasing her from his hold, his breathing ragged, his eyes whispering concern.

'You want to stop—'

'No,' she said hastily, interrupting him. *Never,* she thought silently.

'Because—'

'I know what I want, Loukis. Do you?' she demanded as she stepped back from him, worried that his questions, his second guesses might be the undoing of her.

His dark gaze morphed from concern to absolute conviction. 'Yes. Célia. I know exactly what I want.'

He pinned her with a gaze full of predatory power.

'I want to see you.'

It wasn't a demand, or a statement. It was a wish, one she felt in her very bones. One that lent her a power over Loukis she could never have imagined.

She reached for the fastening at the side of her top and released the tight material binding a chest she wanted to bare to him, to his touch. She drew it over her shoulders and head and cast it aside, relishing the flare in his dark eyes as he took her in, his gaze sweeping over her midnight-blue lace bra, to the skirt at her narrow waist.

All of you.

He didn't have to say it. She felt it as if he had whispered it against her skin. She reached for the zip behind her and drew it down, releasing the band and allowing the silk to drop and pool at her feet. He stood there, as if holding himself back, as if fighting some invisible leash, straining against his desire for her and some last shred of resistance.

She stepped out of the circle of her skirts and walked towards him in her underwear and heels. Never before had she felt so powerful, so attractive, so much herself. She was owning it all, just as much as she was owning her desire for him.

His hands fisted by his sides, still holding himself from her. From what they could have together. Hers went to the buttons on his shirt, slowly releasing them from his neck, down to his waist, pulling at the shirt to release it from his trousers.

He let her push the cotton from his shoulders, until he stood there, shirtless. His body was a marvel of muscle, and she gloried in it, her fingers tracing over dips and swells, causing him to inhale swiftly as he flinched.

When her hands went to the buckle on his belt, it was as if the spell that had held him back had been lifted, and he reached for her, pulling her upward, causing her to wrap her legs around his waist. They sought each other's lips at the same time, the feeling of his tongue crashing against the sensations of skin against skin as he walked them through some darkened maze of furniture she couldn't have navigated.

He brought her to an open part of the living room, the plush soft cream carpet visible in the light of the moon, shafting through large windows that formed the side of the estate.

He laid her down gently, gazing at her from above, and she was unable to take her eyes from him as he made swift work of his trousers. He stood before her naked and glorious, and everything she'd ever wanted.

He came to her then, a kiss full of desire and want, drenching her in a need that she could barely contain. His body against hers, skin against skin, was almost, but not, enough. His fingers snapped the clasp of her bra and he drew the straps down her shoulders and cast it aside. His mouth tracing the path his fingers had made, pressing open-mouthed kisses against her skin, drawing cries of pleasure from her.

She arched into his mouth, his touch, gasped when his fingers found the taut nipple of one breast, then another. His hand swept down her body, between her legs, the firm pressure confident, shocking and devastating to her arousal.

She wished the thin material separating them gone, but his hand swept over her again and again, as if relishing the barrier between them, the last there was to be had, teasing them both on the brink of what they both desperately wanted.

He pressed kisses beneath her breast, trailing down over her stomach, her hip, and lower, to where he pulled at the band of her thong, following the path of its removal with his mouth. At her feet, he removed the scrap of lace, and took up her ankle, delighting in the slow play of undoing the clasp of her shoe, removing one heel and then another.

She looked up at him, knowing she was now completely bare to him.

He reached for his wallet, discarded with his trousers, and sheathed himself with a condom, his eyes not once leaving hers, the promise in them not once faltering.

She expected him to lean forward, to rush towards the end of their pleasure, but he didn't. He trailed his hands up her calves, over her knees and gently pressed at her thighs until her legs lay either side of his where he kneeled before her. His hand returned to between her legs, instinctively causing her to want to draw them together, to hold him to her or hide from him, even she couldn't tell.

She felt his thumb press gently against her clitoris, just held there as if waiting for her to get used to his touch, as if waiting for her to unfurl beneath him. Because that was what it felt like. An unfurling. Her hips shifted, trying to create the pleasurable friction he was withholding, and he smiled, as if knowing exactly what she wanted. His free hand went to her hip, holding her in place there too, and she felt utterly under his command.

He waited until she had stopped, until she had succumbed and then, only then did his fingers start to move. His dark erotic gaze not once leaving hers, as if he wanted to see what he was doing to her, as if it fed his own desire.

His thumb moved over and over and over her clitoris, and her head fell back under the on-slaught of pleasure he was wringing from her. When his fingers entered her she gasped, desperately trying to hold on, desperately clinging to the edge of the precipice she felt herself hurtling towards.

Incomprehensible words, cries, pleas escaped her lips and she was unable to prevent her hips rising, giving him more, wanting more from him. He controlled her, he orchestrated every pleasurable sound and feeling, drawing a shiver of damp heat across her body. Trembling now, she was entirely his, owned, possessed, inside and out.

'Come for me,' he demanded of her. And she did. The waves of ecstasy crashing over her, body and soul wiped clean and mindless to anything other than pleasure.

In all his life, Loukis had never seen anything more beautiful, more humbling. The pink slashes across Célia's cheeks, the erratic rise and fall of her breasts, the way her legs had pulled tight against his thighs as she had reached her orgasm just made him want her more.

A need, painful in its intensity, stung the back of his throat, as he leaned forward to claim her mouth with his. He wanted it all, every gasp, sigh, cry, breath, captured by him. Positioning himself between her legs, he waited until her eyes found his once more. He wanted her with him in this, he wanted to see her as he possessed her, as surely as she had possessed him. When her tiger's eyes met his, desire blackening her gaze, he felt it in his soul.

Slowly, inch by inch, he pressed into her, relishing the incredible feeling of her, his heart stuttering in his chest as she tightened around him, until he could go no further. Just as slowly he withdrew, teasing himself and her. After the frantic pace of their kisses and her orgasm, this slow descent into sensual madness was indescribable and utterly unique to Célia.

Before he could question why, sensations and need welled within him, his body demanding action, demanding more, demanding *now*. But he held himself back, slowly weaving an intoxicating spell as he entered her and withdrew again and again and again.

Her body began to move, showing only a fraction of the restlessness he felt roaring through his body. He captured her mouth with his, before her pleas and moans of pleasure could undo him, drawing out the inevitable moment when their climax would end this. Because he realised he didn't want it to end. He delighted in her pleasure, his no less for it. In fact, his need was heightened by hers.

He felt her hands around his thighs, holding him deep within her, she arching against him as if wringing more and more pleasure from it and no longer could he hold back. He thrust into her deep and fast, her cries of need urging him on, faster, deeper, until he could no longer tell whose cry demanded more, whose pleasure was greater, whose need was more. Until he realised that it didn't matter because, at that moment, they were one.

As if the very thought released the last vestige of his control, an orgasm more powerful, more incredible than any he had ever known roared through them both, calling for hers, demanding hers and together they fell beneath moonbeams and starlight.

CHAPTER TEN

CÉLIA WAS WOKEN by the sounds of conversation, slowly rousing her from the deepest sleep she'd had in years. When her eyes opened, the curtains, the bed beneath her, the partial view from the window jarred painfully.

She rose immediately, her mind taking a moment to catch up. She remembered Loukis picking her up at some point in the night, and bringing her to his bed, where they had once again lost themselves in each other. Her body ached, but it felt strong. She stretched, leaning into the echoes of the sensual pleasure he had drawn from her. A blush rose to her cheeks at the memories from the night before, warming her skin just as a peal of childish giggles filtered from down the hall.

Annabelle.

She cast a glance around the room, suddenly very conscious that she was naked. Wrapping the sheet around her, she left the bed and padded over to the wardrobe carefully concealed behind mirrors that had teased and taunted them last night as they had…

Célia cut the train of thought in its tracks. She pulled open a door, hoping to find something of Loukis's that she could wear, but once she caught sight of the contents she stopped, hovering in shock. The clothes she had chosen from the stylist lined the length of the hanging rail, shoes tucked neatly at the bottom, drawers—she saw as she pulled them open—full of underwear.

'You will share my bed.'

Last night had been her decision. And she had known that this was part of the bargain they had struck. But what did that mean for the forthcoming evening? And the evenings after?

As Célia showered, she was torn between concerns for the future and the heady memories of last night, her body certainly desirous of another night spent in his arms. Arms that had held her as she'd had the most powerful sexual experience of her life. Marc had been dutiful in bed with her, as if it were something 'to be done'. And she could see now that even that was part of Marc's plan. It wasn't and never had been about her, but what she could give him.

And no matter how differently Loukis saw her, treated her, she was still exactly the same to him. She could give him the reputation and the situation he needed for Annabelle. She couldn't, wouldn't let her heart make another mistake and think for a second it was about anything else. Hadn't Loukis himself said as much?

'I am not capable of giving you what you deserve. Not now. Not ever.'

She hated that the deepest irony was that it was Loukis that deserved more. Because she *wasn't* the perfect fiancée he needed. She could never risk him finding out the truth of what had happened with her father. Not only because of the damage it could do to his custody claim…but the damage she feared it could do to her.

After showering and dressing Célia made her way down the hall, towards the sounds coming from what she could only assume was a kitchen or dining room. It turned out to be both. A beautiful sprawling open kitchen and eating area backed by the most gorgeous view of the Greek island where Loukis had made his summer home.

The moment Annabelle caught sight of her, she jumped up from the table, rushed around and came to a startling halt about two feet from where Célia stood. A shy, but utterly thrilled expression on her face.

'Hi!'

'Bonjour, ma chérie.'

'I told you she'd call me Cherry,' she cried victoriously to Loukis, before rushing up the stairs in the far corner with indistinguishable words about wanting 'to show Célia'.

Célia finally looked to her fiancé. Her *fake* fiancé. He was studying her over the rim of the small espresso cup he held to his lips, stopped just before he could take a sip.

She met his eyes and her heart thudded wildly in her chest. His gaze was proprietorial as if, unspoken, he had claimed her. As if he knew that she knew it too. It was full of promise, of heat, reminding her of what he had whispered to her in the night. Of the things he wanted to do to her, for her, instantly igniting an arousal, a need, that only he could meet.

'Good morning,' Loukis said, his tone as rough and deep as her thoughts.

She nodded and took a seat opposite him at the table, forcing her eyes to the view from the window, rather than the one in front of her.

'Sleep well?' he asked, a smile playing at the lips that had ravished her for hours the night before.

As if the gentle taunt called forth some of the power she had felt that night, she replied, 'Very. And you?'

'Not so much. I was distracted a little by a—'

'Here! Look,' Annabelle said, rushing back into the room and dumping something small and

fluffy on Célia's lap, cutting through the under-
currents of their exchange like a knife through
butter.

'It's Mr Cat,' Annabelle said proudly of the
distinctly dog-like toy.

'Mr Cat,' Célia repeated. 'Nice to meet you,'
she said, taking the strange fluffy figure's paw
between her thumb and finger, shaking it in
greeting, and trying hard to stifle the shocked,
choking sound coming from Loukis.

'What happened to Jameson?' Loukis asked.

'He lives with Mummy. But Mr Cat can live
with you,' Annabelle stated, seemingly ignorant
of the slight flinch that shook Loukis's body.
'We're going to the beach today,' Annabelle announced, clearly of a mind that Célia would be
in attendance. She was torn. Part of her wanted
to spend the day whiling away the hours with
Loukis and Annabelle, and the other wanted to
hide, to retreat into work for the day, putting as
much emotional distance between them as possible. Because this happy family unit...it was
both tempting and terrifying.

Loukis had sensed Célia's hesitation at the breakfast table, but refused to feel guilty at joining
Annabelle in her not so gentle persuasion. Pro-
tests about not having a costume were refuted
by the simple fact he had made sure that there

was swimwear included in her new wardrobe. Objections based on work had been cast aside as it was a Sunday. Unable to prevent himself, any further refusals were silenced by a quick, firm kiss on her lips, which had apparently delighted Annabelle, whose enthusiastic squeals were punctuated by fist pumps and cries of 'yes', and shocked Célia into agreement.

Perhaps he had underestimated his little sister's happy expectations and he refused to think of the time when that would come to a natural conclusion after the custody hearing. Because he was beginning to see Célia as more than a means to an end. Though what that actually meant eluded him.

For so many years he had remained firmly unattached. Determinedly so. Convinced that any kind of relationship was based on nothing more than delusional romantic notions that simply aligned with financial avarice, sexual desire and, on occasion, pregnancy—unexpected or otherwise.

But as he watched Annabelle and Célia play in the surf, the rolling waves crashing against the private beach, the sun-kissed skin across Célia's shoulders and the happy smile on his sister's face, he was beginning to understand the appeal. Walls were shifting within him as he felt a sense of something greater than himself and his goal of custody. But that only served to make him disconcerted, his natural inclination to turn away from a lifelong-held belief that would not be shaken by one night.

Not that it would be one night, he realised. Not now that he'd had an exquisite taste of Célia.

Annabelle had finally grown tired of handstands and underwater somersaults and made her way to where he sat ready and waiting with towels, drinks and, more importantly to his sister, crisps. Behind her, Célia seemed to drag her feet, as if reluctant to return to the tactile interaction of yesterday. Of before.

He made space for them to sit on the large beach blanket they'd brought with them, noticing that Annabelle seemed distracted as she wasn't head down in the packet of crisps.

'Nanny? You okay?'

She sighed in a way that made her sound much older than her ten years. 'If I…if the custurdy thing says I have to go and live with Mummy, what happens to you?'

Despite Annabelle's mispronunciation, it was on his lips to deny that she would ever go and live with Meredith, but he caught Célia's focused look. As if she knew what he was about to say and desperate for him to change it. He'd done and was doing everything in his power to ensure that the custody case went his way, but he wouldn't make a promise to her that he might not be able to keep. He remembered what Célia had said that evening after the video call. He remembered her warning to be there as a support for Annabelle and had taken it to heart.

'Annabelle, no matter what happens, who the courts decide you will live with, there will always be a safe place for you here with me.'

His answer didn't seem to solve whatever his sister was wrestling with.

'If you're worried, I'll do my best to make sure that what you want is heard.'

To his horror, tears glowed within Annabelle's eyes.

'But…what if…what if I don't know what I want?'

'What do you mean, *chérie*?' Célia asked, putting her arm around Annabelle's shoulders.

'What if I don't know who I want to be with?' Annabelle whispered, looking at Célia as if she was too fearful to look at him.

Pain cut through Loukis. Pain and anger at his mother. Anger that Meredith had caused so much confusion and hurt in his sister. Because all he could see was having to pick up the pieces. Again. Of the eventual moment that his mother abandoned her. Again. And deeper than that, the ache with which he viewed his future without the little girl who had come to mean so much to him.

Célia looked up at him then, as if willing him to say the right thing. There was compassion in her gaze, too, but that seemed to hurt just as much. He forced the words to his lips. 'Annabelle, if you would like to live with your mother—'

'No! Well, maybe? I don't know.'

'And that's okay, sweetheart,' insisted Célia. 'Even adults don't always know what they want. You had fun with Meredith in Texas?'

'Yes, but I have fun here with Loukis too.'

'I can see,' she said, smiling. 'And your friends…'

'Are here. At school and Leya—she's my bestest friend.'

'Byron seems nice,' Célia pressed on while Loukis didn't feel capable of forming words at all.

'He is. He laughs a lot and has a funny accent.'

'And your mummy?'

Loukis marvelled that Célia was managing to bring out exactly the information that he wanted from his sister, who shrugged and seemed to burrow into herself.

'I don't know.'

Célia laughed gently, breaking some of the tension gripping both Loukis and his sister in a fierce hold.

'I haven't known how to feel about my dad for nearly five years,' she confided.

'Really?' Annabelle returned, wide-eyed.

'*Really.* There are times when I remember good things. Happy things. And times when, I know that he made me sad. Sometimes they get mixed up together and sometimes they feel very far apart.'

It was, Célia realised, the first time that she'd admitted to feeling something other than betrayal from her father. Ever. But that didn't stop it from being true. She had loved, *did* love him. But that love had been damaged by his betrayal and she could only imagine that being half of what Annabelle might be feeling, and at ten she quite possibly had no idea how to explain that. Especially to Loukis who, until recently, had simply pushed through with determination to ensure that Meredith came nowhere near her.

'Do you still speak to him?' Annabelle asked.

'Not for quite a while.'

'And your mummy?'

Célia sighed, and smiled, not realising quite how sad she looked in that moment. 'We've spoken more recently.'

'I spoke to my mum yesterday. She looked pretty and said she was going to your party.'

'Nanny.' Loukis waited until he had his sister's attention and Célia's. He seemed to be struggling with what he had to say. 'No matter what happens, I will always be here for you. No matter where you are in the world, or who you are with. You are my family. Nothing will ever change that.'

Célia felt as if a giant bell had been struck within her and as it swung back and forth, shivering tremors in its wake, her heart lurched in time and in tune. They were the words she had never heard, nor felt from her own father, let alone her ex-fiancé. But to hear them from Loukis's lips made her want, made her ache to hear them spoken for her. By him. She looked away at the horizon where the sea met the sky to avoid Loukis's penetrating gaze. He would see, he would know.

As she'd watched him with Annabelle, seeing him with his friends Yalena and Iannis, and with her own, Ella and Roman, Loukis had morphed from an irascible client, a renowned playboy, into something more, *someone* more.

'I am not capable of giving you what you deserve. Not now. Not ever.'

'But you don't like her,' she heard Annabelle announce, even as Célia focused on a small fishing boat further out in the sea.

'How I feel about her doesn't affect how *you* feel about her, and it won't affect how...*she* feels about you.'

The conclusion of Loukis's sentence felt forced, but her heart soared that he was trying. Trying to present a blank canvas for his sister, so that she might be able to forge a relationship with her mother that was positive, even as she knew he would hate that.

But, as with all things that flew too high, they had to come down, and Célia's heart swooped when she realised that his words reminded her of her last conversation with her mother.

Célia had demanded to know why her mother had sided with her father. Why she couldn't seem to understand how betrayed and lost Célia felt and why she wasn't there for her.

'He is my husband, Célia. If I held him accountable for every little—'

'Little? You're saying this is little?'

'Non, ma fille. Pas du tout. *But over the years we have both made mistakes...parental ones. He has forgiven me mine as I forgive him his. Because my feelings for him, whether you like it or not, are separate from my feelings for you. One day, I hope, you will understand these mistakes and that they were not intended—'*

'This wasn't just a mistake, Maman. It was an act. An intentional, business-focused act that took my idea and used it for the most atrocious means.'

*'And those "atrocious means" have funded our
entire lives until now, Célia. You can't deny—'*

'Célia?'

She looked up to find Loukis standing above
her, his body blocking out the powerful sun, the
items they had brought with them to the beach
packed up and even Annabelle standing ready
to leave.

Had she been the one in the wrong? Had she
reacted to her mother's response and drawn a
line in the sand between herself and her parents
from her words? Célia had been so hurt and so
betrayed, had spent so long feeling unloved and
unwanted that it had felt as if her mother had
chosen her father. But looking back on it now,
she realised that her mother had been trying to
tell her that she loved her and Célia was the one
to reject that love. Suddenly it seemed absolutely
vital that she speak to her mother. Now, before
she could talk herself out of it.

'Why don't you go on? I'll join you in a bit.'

Loukis's gaze showed confusion and something almost like concern, but he nodded and
took Annabelle's hand. She watched them make
their way back up to the house before reaching
for her phone with trembling fingers.

Something had happened on the beach. What exactly it was, Loukis couldn't be sure, but Célia

was…different. Lighter? Her laughter mingled with Annabelle's and it sounded, felt, freer somehow. The looks she cast his way were unguarded, and what he saw in her eyes was beginning to burn through the barriers around his heart.

For the first time ever, he wanted more. More than the façade of a fake fiancée. More than just one night with her. More than just the time limit he'd placed on their relationship. He wanted long dinners with friends, wanted to show her the places he loved to visit, wanted to see her eyes widen with wonder and feel the rich sound of her beautiful laugh roll over his naked skin.

It had been a constant whisper throughout the day, seductive and enticing. But he wouldn't, couldn't, give into it. The custody hearing was only a few days away and he had to keep his focus on that.

But after? his internal voice teased. *What then?*

Over dinner he'd been distracted by images of a future with Célia, of years not months, of days as well as nights. Of her growing round with his child, of a family he'd never thought he'd want.

That was why he'd spent at least an hour in his study, after Célia had gone to bed. Because if he'd gone with her, he couldn't honestly say what he would have done. What he would have begged for, pleaded for. It was a weakness. It could be exploited. He'd done so only once in his life and he'd learned his lesson then and there. Everything had a price. Even love could be bought. His mother's certainly had. And the only price he could afford to pay at the moment was Annabelle's. Nothing more.

He glanced at the clock. Surely by now Célia would be asleep and he could persevere through the fresh torture of having her in his bed and not touching her. Even the thought of it sent need directly to his groin. Even the memory of the sounds she had made the night before drove an arousal so fierce he nearly shook with the need to restrain it. Just the thought of the delicious taste of her was enough to have him swallow the last inch of whiskey in an attempt to blot out the yearning to taste her again.

Enough. He had more control over himself than this. He could and would leave her untouched this night. And as if to prove it to himself, he stalked determinedly down the hallway towards his bedroom.

Two strides into the room, stealthily as humanly possible, the bedside lamp flicked light across the room and revealed that Célia was very much awake and very much expecting him.

'Thought I'd be asleep?' she asked, no censure or accusation in her tone, just curiosity and that openness that had taunted him all afternoon.

'Hoped,' he said with something like a grimace pulling at his features.

'Because?'

'Because I'd wanted to avoid this,' he replied honestly.

'My conversation is so terrifying to you that it kept you from your bed?'

He sat on the side of the bed, his back to her momentarily as he pulled off his shoes and reached for his belt. As his fingers gripped it, he remembered last night, he remembered everything.

'I spoke to my mother this afternoon.'

Her words struck him still. Frowning, he turned to look at her, searching for traces of hurt or sadness. The swift desire to protect her from any source of pain shocking him with its intensity.

'How did it go?' he couldn't help himself from asking.

She looked sad and happy at the same time. Both caused a shifting sensation in his chest. Her beautiful amber eyes were glistening with tears, but the smile across her lips was sure.

'Good. It was…' she sighed '…good. And I wanted to thank you.'

'Why?' Loukis replied, genuinely confused.

'I wouldn't have made that phone call had it

not been for what you said, what you did, for Annabelle today.'

He felt the invisible tendrils wound tight around his heart begin to unfurl, even as he would call them back.

'I did only as you suggested,' he dismissed.

'But you gave her, you gave *me*, the space within which we could find…peace. Safety. I want you to know that.'

'I don't—'

'Please don't dismiss this,' she asked.

His jaw clenched, anger and something like fear rearing their heads at her words. He stood and started to stalk towards the bathroom.

'Wait. Please?'

He stopped, but refused to turn, bracing himself for what he knew was to come.

'I think… I think that it might be what you are doing too.'

He rounded on her then. 'One conversation with *your* mother convinces you that you know *me*? That you know my—' He cut himself off before he could release the word he refused to admit to.

'Pain? The pain of being ignored by a parent? Of being rejected?'

'I wasn't ignored by my mother, Célia. She chose to leave. She chose to accept the money my father offered her in exchange for sole custody.'

'What?' she asked, horror dawning in her eyes as her hand flew to her mouth as if to stifle a gasp.

'Ten million euros. That was the price my mother accepted to be free of me. I had no culpability in that whatsoever. It was not my doing, my offer, or my suggestion.' Because there was no financial amount that would have made him reject his mother. No matter what highs or lows she had inflicted on him. *That* was the weakness he feared. *That* was the bitter truth he'd realised about himself that day. That he would have done anything to keep her with him. Anything. And Meredith had done nothing.

'No. You're right. It wasn't your doing, Loukis.'

'I know that. I just said—'

'Do you?'

It infuriated him that she was so calm. She could have been talking about the weather. Her gentle words were tearing gaping holes in his heart and she sat there poised and perfect.

'Do you really?' she asked again. 'Or, deep down, do you blame yourself?'

'What do you want me to say, Célia? You want me to say that I didn't learn, at the age of fifteen, my value was ten million euros? That it didn't hurt to be sold to my father in exchange for her freedom? To admit that I wasn't enough to keep her?'

The words were ripped from his throat, burning and tearing at the soft flesh, making his tone guttural and harsh, even to his own ears.

'No. I want you to admit that you *do* deserve more. That you *are* worthy of her love.'

That you are worthy of mine, his greedy, desperate inner voice filled in the silence between her words.

'You might not be ready to and that's okay. But I want you to know that I think you are. Worthy. Of that, of more than what you have limited yourself to.'

He turned back towards the bathroom, his jaw clenched so hard, he feared he might crack a tooth. His fists balled where they hung at his sides, the pulse raging through his blood so loud it blocked out the sound of her leaving the bed and coming up behind him, so that when he felt her hand on his shoulder he flinched.

He let himself be pulled around to face her. Let her seek out his gaze, unable to shutter the effect her words had had on him.

'I see so much when I look at you, Loukis. I see—'

He cut off her words with a kiss fuelled with need, pain and want. Need for her, pain for himself and want for what he couldn't have. Because he couldn't, wouldn't hear the words that would follow. The promise of feelings, of love, he believed she wouldn't be able to fulfil, for the sheer simple fact that no one else in his life had done so. Not his mother, nor his father, changed for ever after his wife's betrayal. And if they couldn't…

His chaotic thoughts veered away from the darkness as a starburst of light burned through him at her touch, at the way her hands—placed either side of his face—anchored him to her, focusing him on her.

How did she do this? How did she take his hurt and wash over it with acceptance and more? How did she see to the heart of him, yet join him rather than abandon him? The answer, he feared, would be more devastating than any lie he could tell himself. Because if she could love him, then why hadn't his parents? Somehow that thought only compounded the pain. All of it.

Within the kiss, her tongue teased, and fingers taunted, the little moans of pleasure falling from her lips found safe haven within him as he greedily consumed everything she had to give, despite his thoughts and fears.

He was done roasting himself over hot coals, the sensual web Célia was weaving drawing him in deeper to her, demanding more. Demanding everything. And as he laid her back on the bed, he feared that he would do it. Pay any damn price for everything she had to offer.

CHAPTER ELEVEN

DURING THE COURSE of the week on the island, Célia had worked a magic over Loukis that he couldn't account for. Under her steady gaze, full of a confidence in something he didn't want to put name to, a sense of rightness that he'd never felt before settled in his chest.

It was for this, and this reason only, that he got out of the limousine, stalked round the back of the car, and opened Célia's car door with a smile full and secure despite the fact that they were about to walk into a court hearing where he would confront his mother. He knew, he *felt*, that it would all be okay. That the courts would see Meredith for who she truly was—the person who had abandoned not one, but two children, the person who was clearly only interested in playing at being a mother to secure a rich American fiancé with strong family values—and that he could put the whole thing behind him and move forward. Move forward with Annabelle *and* Célia.

She looked glorious today. In a russet-coloured dress that veed between her breasts and tied at her hip, the silk pouring over her gorgeous shapely legs. It wasn't overtly sexy, more…confident and assured. He loved seeing her like this. He loved the way her eyes flared as she placed her hand in his, the promise in them echoing from the night before and leading towards the night to come.

They met his lawyers at the entranceway to the building and made their introductions, before being led into a small office within the building that they had been assigned for preparation and briefings.

Never ones for wasting their obscenely expensive time, his lawyers got right down to business, outlining the way that the day would run, the rules and regulations of the court for Célia's benefit. Although they were in Greece, with so many English-speaking individuals involved the proceedings would be undertaken with a translator present if needed.

They outlined the strategies to counter the areas of contention, his reputation, the natural leaning for the court to side with the mother, both being met by his new engagement, and Meredith's previous patterns of behaviour. As Loukis's fiancée and therefore someone who would be a very important part of Annabelle's life and upbringing, she would be providing a character statement not only for Loukis, but of herself. They were scheduled for just before lunch and until then Célia would be able to sit in the gallery. Even though it was a closed hearing, in order to protect Annabelle from the intense public interest, the associated individuals were allowed to stay.

'And your investigators haven't been able to find anything on Byron?' he asked, hopeful of perhaps this last reprieve.

'Clean as a whistle. He's exactly who he appears to be. A rich oil baron, longing for a family and desperately in love with your—with Meredith. Loukis, I know that you had expected to receive a financial request from her. I'm assuming you haven't?'

'No,' he said grimly.

'Shame. It would have made things easier. But I'm confident that the judge will find for us.'

He felt Célia's hand reach for his, entwining her fingers with his, and the pad of his thumb brushed over her engagement ring. Suddenly he thought it *was* a shame. A shame that he had given her such a beautiful ring for show and not for her.

He shook his head. He needed to focus. There

would be time. Time for Célia and for them later. Now, he needed to head his mother off at the pass.

'Ready?' demanded the lawyer.

With one last glance at Célia, who was glorious with belief and assurance ringing her eyes, he stood. 'I'm ready.'

Despite outward appearances, Célia was worried. It was only when she took her seat behind the table where Loukis and his lawyers faced the judge that she allowed her mask to slip a little. She knew that Loukis needed her assurance, her faith so she had given it freely. But she hadn't missed the way that Loukis had almost unfurled in the time spent on the island, relaxed into the strange unspoken forward step their relationship had taken.

The night after her conversation with her mother had been like the last burst of a dam, the water punching through its final barrier. They had spoken for a long time, and Célia had tried to explain what she'd been feeling then, why she'd reacted the way she had. And her mother had told her how she might have disagreed with her husband but was trying to love them both in her own way. And Célia had finally accepted that love. And with that had come the realisation that she loved Loukis. She had felt it, she had wanted to tell him then that she had fallen for him. For the wonderful, incredible man she saw when she looked at him. But he had prevented her words and at the time she had understood. But in the days that followed, his excitement, the eager anticipation for the forthcoming custody hearing, the little verbal slips he made in suggesting plans that reached beyond this point, beyond their allotted few months of engagement, had made her hope.

And it was that hope that scared her. Because she knew that she would have to tell him. Tell him the truth of what her designs had been used for. Only then would she be truly free to love and be loved. She had to trust that he would accept her. All of her, including her imperfections. She wanted it so much, she ached.

'All rise.'

After all the carefully orchestrated publicity stunts, the engagement party, the perfectly cultivated relationship between them, the court hearing seemed oddly mundane. The introductions by the judge and each of the lawyers held a patterned rhythm of formal decorum that swept away the early morning hours and all the while, Célia couldn't help but think of what Annabelle would be doing with her friend Leya. They had planned to visit the park and then the zoo, Annabelle now fixated on a future as a vet.

As Loukis took the stand Célia cast a look towards Meredith and Byron, the latter catching her gaze and producing a smile full of warmth, completely at odds with the antagonism palpable between Meredith and her son. Haltingly she smiled back, Meredith catching the shared glance and frowning before something passed across her features. Something almost victorious.

Nervously she focused her attention back to the answers Loukis was giving to his own lawyers. He outlined the existing housing and care he was providing for Annabelle, letting them guide his answers to how difficult and traumatic it had been for her to be abandoned by her mother. The raw pain he expressed at his initial feelings of helplessness at his sister's misery was felt by all. To her credit, a pale Meredith seemed contrite and distraught to hear of it. His lawyers didn't miss a single thing that would give them an edge over the opposing counsel.

It was Meredith's lawyers' turn next, probing gently at his own feelings towards Meredith, suggesting that perhaps it was his own abandonment that had coloured his feelings over the situation. Célia's heart pounded in her chest to see him so exposed, but to her surprise they seemed sympathetic towards him. Not even touching on his own reputation. Something that even Loukis seemed surprised by.

By the time they indicated that they had no

further questions, Loukis, his lawyers and Célia were confused. All of their attention had been so focused on defending assumed attack from that quarter, the sheer fact that they hadn't gone down that path made it seem as if they didn't even want to win the case.

'Ms d'Argent? If you would?'

Célia took a deep breath, gratefully received a supportive smile from Loukis and made her way towards the chair to the right of the judge. Focusing on answering Loukis's lawyers' questions helped some of the nerves Célia felt rising within her, ebbing and flowing, sometimes jerking at the spike of adrenaline when she had to pause and consider her words and how they might be interpreted by the opposition. But she answered them truthfully. Yes, she had met Loukis through work, but that relationship had developed. Yes, she had met Annabelle and taken the lovely little girl into her heart. No, she didn't have personal experience in parenting, but understood what it would mean for her future with Loukis if he were to become guardian of Annabelle and was one hundred per cent in support of it and was looking forward to being in her life. Yes, she had relocated to Greece to be with him, and most definitely yes thought that Loukis would be a wonderful parent.

With their thanks for her time, Loukis's lawyers sat down and Meredith's stood.

'Ms d'Argent, you have not always been CEO of Chariton Endeavours, have you?'

'No, the company was formed three years ago with Ella Black, a school friend.'

'And before that?'

'Before Chariton?'

'Yes.'

Célia shrugged. 'I was at university in Paris.'

'And what did you study there?'

'A degree in Humanities and—'

'But you started out with a different degree, no?'

Célia frowned, her heart beginning to pound in her chest. She cast a glance towards Meredith, to see a vindictive edge to her gaze. She *knew*. She turned to Loukis, wanting him to make it stop, needing him to. Because if he didn't, Loukis would lose everything and it would be her fault. A cold sweat broke out across her shoulder blades, sending shivers along her skin.

'Ms d'Argent? Please answer the question.'

'I… My university education began with a degree in mathematics and computer sciences.'

'And it was that which led you to an internship with Paquet Industries.'

Although Célia was looking at the lawyer, she saw Loukis lean to the man next to him, a frown marking his features, and confusion emanating from their table.

I'm so sorry, Loukis.

Fear and rage welled within her, for him, for herself. She knew she should have told him. Told him the true extent of what her father had done with her plans. But she'd thought those records were sealed. That no one would ever find out.

'Yes,' she said meekly.

'And while you were there, you had worked on technical specifications for a missile guidance system.'

'No.'

The lawyer's eyes blazed with the same intensity as Meredith's had, as if sensing victory.

'Need I remind you that even though this is a custody hearing, anything you say must be the truth, or it will be seen as perjury?'

'You do not. The specifications I was working on were for drone guidance systems for agricultural use in developing countries,' she said shakily.

'There is no record of that.'

'Those records are sealed.'

'Which might have been the case five years ago, but six months ago, François Paquet licensed the patent for his missile technology under IEPRA guidelines and as such they became a matter of public record.'

All Célia could hear was the roar of her own pulse. She felt as if her chest were about to explode.

'So. Do you deny that you developed technical specifications for a drone missile system that has been sold by Paquet Industries—an international defence contractor—and used to take the lives of nearly four thousand people across the globe?'

Noise filled the room. Objections and cries of shock from Loukis's legal team, the judge's gavel pounding on the wood behind her in time with the raging of her own heart, and above all Meredith's shrill voice, proclaiming she would not allow a *murderer* to care for her daughter.

Célia's field of vision narrowed to her hands, shaking and suddenly frigidly cold. Her breaths were coming in short sharp pants and nausea gripped her stomach in a fierce hold.

She vaguely found herself pulled from the chair, Loukis's concerned face hazy, snatching glances at people who were staring at her, imagining their faces twisted in horror, as she was led from the room and back to the small office where they had started this day.

Murderer.

What the hell was going on? Loukis fisted his hands, wanting to lash out at something. Anything. Célia was hunched over in the chair he had poured her into. His legal team filled the room looking as concerned as he was. But in all likelihood their concern was focused on the custody case now completely hijacked from the last source he had ever expected it to come from.

But his mind fractured. He had seen Célia begin to tremble, still sitting by the judge. The way her skin had paled and he'd known. Known something awful was about to happen and he'd not been able to do a damn thing to stop it.

Snippets of conversations filtered through his mind.

'It was taken from me...'

'Very good at "the computer science thing"...'

'Used in a very different way from what I had intended...'

'I will not allow a murderer to care for my daughter...'

Someone was telling Célia to breathe and a distant part of him recognised that it should have been him. Him making sure she was okay. But he was held in a vortex of shock and fear. They should have known something was wrong when Meredith's legal team didn't go after him for all the things they had suspected they would. They didn't need to. Because they had Célia. His mother had used Célia to bring him to his knees.

At that precise moment, Célia finally looked up at him. Her eyes glistening with unshed tears, her breath finally coming back to some semblance of normality.

'Leave us,' he demanded of the lawyers. As if sensing the storm brewing, they filed out of the room leaving Célia and Loukis alone.

'Loukis—'

'Explain what just happened to me.'

'I...'

'I can't do this for you, Célia. I have no idea what just happened. So just...tell me.'

'My father took the technical specifications from me and used them to bolster the designs for Paquet's combat drone. One that has since been sold around the world as one of the top ten UAVs available—'

'UAV?' he interrupted.

'Unmanned Aerial Vehicle.'

'So they were right?'

'Loukis, I didn't do it,' she pleaded. 'My designs were never intended for combat or the defence industry. I had no idea—'

'But they are right.'

'Yes.'

'Why the hell didn't you tell me?' he roared, unable to hold himself back. Everything he'd done, all of it, to protect his sister, it was slipping through his fingers like sand.

'Because I thought the records were sealed.

the designs.'

'Just how naïve are you? It's a legal patent. Of course he would have had to put your name down on the paperwork.'

He was half convinced that he was now shaking as much as Célia. Only he was furious. And she was scared, he realised, desperately attempting to pull back on the leash that had been lifted from his anger. He was going to lose. He was going to lose Annabelle. And Célia...

'I didn't tell you because I was ashamed. Because I know what those drones have done and will continue to do. Why do you think I was so determined to counter that with the charity work I do?'

'Well, it's not like I would have been able to guess that with you keeping so many damn secrets.' The line was petty and he hated himself for it, but couldn't stop it.

'I didn't tell you,' she said finally, in the softest of voices, 'because you wanted the perfect fiancée. You didn't, in fact, want someone whose reputation is worse than your own.'

He couldn't deny her words. He knew she was telling the truth. That she had believed no one would find out. And he could see that she was destroyed by the revelation in court, by the knowledge of what her designs had been put to use for. But did it matter? Right now, to the granting of guardianship over Annabelle?

He turned away from her then, unable to bear the weight of her watery eyes. Each glint cut against him, burying into his heart, exposing a raw pain, a deeper truth. One that could not be denied. All this time he'd roared and railed against the pain of being abandoned, rejected in favour of money. His father left a broken shell by the divorce and never quite fully recovering. And Loukis, himself, left horrified and damaged by the knowledge of his worth in his mother's eyes.

But now this time, it was he who was being forced to make the choice. It felt as if he were being torn in two, a painful wrenching that he feared he might never soothe. Neither option would provide enough to compensate for what he would lose.

His mind worked furiously, trying to forecast the outcome of whatever his next move was, until he was dizzy with an infinite number of futures, all of which left him sacrificing something vital to him.

Fury raged within him as he realised that the price he would have to pay for Annabelle was Célia. This beautiful, impassioned, kind, supportive woman who had snuck beneath every single defence he had. And he couldn't have her. Not if he wanted to protect Annabelle from their mother.

* * *

Célia could see it. The moment that he realised what she, herself, had come to realise as soon as Meredith had cried out the word *murderer*. There was no way that she could stay. She was now the greatest threat to his guardianship over Annabelle. A far worse threat than any that Loukis could have represented, or even foreseen.

Loukis's chance at being granted custody had hung by a gossamer thread already. And she had effectively severed that thread. If she stayed.

'Don't,' he commanded as if hearing her thoughts.

'It's the only way.'

He didn't speak, but he was shaking his head as if refusing to listen. Refusing to do the only thing left to do.

She took a deep breath that trembled within her lungs. Oh, it hurt. So, so much. In her mind rose Loukis's words from the first night they had made love. Speaking them now, with her tongue, the words on her lips, she felt them down to her very soul.

'I am not capable of giving you what you deserve. Not now. Not ever.'

'That is not fair.'

'None of it is fair Loukis.'

She looked at him, his hair a chaotic mess, his eyes blazing, torn, but she could tell he knew, could tell that he would not stop her. And even in that, he looked glorious to her. The man who had given her strength, the man who had returned her sense of self to her. The man she had come to love. The man she was now destroying.

The horror she felt rising within her at the sheer fact that she had accidentally brought this down on him was acute. That she was the one who had unconsciously betrayed him... She knew that precise poison betrayal could be, the self-recrimination, anger and helplessness when wishes, plans and hopes for the future were taken away and smashed against the floor. She knew the devastating anguish that would reap for Loukis and she wouldn't, couldn't, do that to him.

'You will return to the court, be as outraged as you like. You didn't know. You would never have allowed me any contact with Annabelle had you known. And you have severed our...connection. I will not be an impediment to your guardianship over Annabelle.'

He said nothing, staring at her so intently she had to break their gaze. Had to because she simply couldn't bear it.

'I'll go straight to the airport. You can send my things on and I'll give you the money—'

'Stop,' he commanded.

'No. Because I'm right and you know it. It's the only way.'

'Célia,' he begged, and she couldn't stand it. 'I can't—'

'I know,' she said, shaking her head, hoping to prevent more excruciating words. 'I understand, Loukis. Truly.'

She got up from the chair, her legs still a little shaky, but forcing the strength that he had given her into her body, heart and soul. She reached for her bag. 'I think you might have been right,' she said with a sad smile. 'Everything *does* have a price. And, Loukis, this is the one that *I* am willing to pay. For you. For Annabelle.

She turned to walk away, but a hand caught her wrist, pulling her back round to him, causing her to crash against his chest. His lips were on hers in an instant, demanding, punishing, as if trying to bend her to his will. His hands came around her face as if trying to anchor her to him, to keep her with him. And it hurt. The agony of what she was doing nearly buckled her. This one last time, this one last kiss, it was too much.

Weak as she was, she reached for him too. Her hands fisting in his shirt, clinging to him, to this moment as if wanting it all and knowing that it would never be enough. At first, she had flinched from his touch, then she had borne it and now she craved it with every fibre of her being. The only way she could find the strength to walk away from him was knowing that to stay would damage him irrevocably.

His thumb swept away a tear she hadn't even realised she'd shed. The bittersweet taste of his kiss haunted her and would continue to haunt her, she knew, for many, many days to come. She broke the kiss and gazed up into his rich dark eyes, but the sea of emotions storming within them was too much.

She left his embrace, turned and left the room, left the court building and blindly hailed a cab. All the while absolutely sure that she had left behind her heart.

CHAPTER TWELVE

By the time his lawyers came to find him in the court's small office, where Célia had left him, some unfathomable amount of time later, he could barely speak. They explained that a recess had been granted, but that it would be at least another five days before the case could be resumed. According to them, Meredith had not been pleased by the news and had nearly been admonished by the judge for her outburst. Even some minor victory over Meredith hadn't been able to shake him. They had put him in his car, and he'd even been blind to the concerned looks they shared between themselves as they sent him off to his estate in Athens.

Having to explain to Annabelle what had happened nearly eviscerated him as his little sister's eyes had welled, just like Célia's, and she'd run away too. He'd known how she'd felt at that moment, wanting himself to hide and lick wounds yet again inflicted by his mother. Though these particular wounds had a sense of self-infliction he just couldn't shake.

So many times in the last three days, he'd wanted to reach out to Célia. Wanted to call her, to see her, but with his lawyers on damage limitation, Annabelle nearly heartbroken at Célia's absence and the insecurity of the looming custody hearing, he barely found the time to eat, let alone sleep.

He was exhausted. He'd not been back to his room since Célia had left. The scent she'd left on his pillows, in the air of the room, he wanted to both avoid it and hoard it at the same time.

But it was more than that. He'd made his choice, that had been unquestionable. But living with it? Again and again he questioned how Célia had come to impact his life so much. Almost daily he wondered what she was wearing— if she had gone back to her beige T-shirt that he'd honestly give anything to see at that moment, or whether she'd continued to wear the beautiful bright clothing that brought out the colours of her eyes and hair. He wondered if she had spoken more with her mother, a reconciliation that he knew would be so healing for her. He missed the simple touches that passed between them as much as the deep passion that drove them to impossible sensual heights, a thirst that he had not come close to quenching.

More than all those things, though, he missed the way she would question him, challenge him to be better, to do more, to think his actions through. He couldn't shake the feeling that he was failing. Epically. Especially when it came to Annabelle.

He wanted her to tell him how to fix it. She had always seemed to know.

He heard the patter of Annabelle's bare feet on the marble staircase and waited until her pyjama-clad little self came into view.

Frowning at the clock, which read eleven-thirty, he turned. 'Everything okay, Nanny?'

Her little hands twisted in front of her, her eyes bruised by lack of sleep.

'Is Célia a bad person?'

Shock sliced through him and he had to bite out the demand for her to explain, forcing himself to think through the words Célia might have said in that moment.

'Why would you think that?' he asked, trying to keep his voice level.

'Mummy said she did a bad thing and that's why she had to go away.'

Every primal instinct to deny, to vent the sudden and shocking fury he felt, roared through him.

'No, sweetheart. She didn't do a bad thing. She…invented something that people used for bad things, but no. Absolutely not. Célia isn't bad at all.'

'Then, can you tell Mummy that so Célia can come back?'

Loukis forced a smile to his features. 'I…' He was about to explain that he had told Meredith, that he had defended Célia, when he realised that he hadn't. There had been no defence of Célia, not in the court and not since. Something twisted in his belly then. Something acidic and harsh and painful.

'You're right, Annabelle. I should do that. But I'm not sure that it would bring Célia back.'

'Why not?'

'Because Meredith doesn't want Célia to live with me while you're here. And sadly the judge might agree.'

'Then I… I think I should go and live with Mummy.'

'Is that something you want to do?' he asked, his voice level and compassionate even as everything in him trembled and shook.

Annabelle frowned. 'No,' she said, shaking her head. 'But then Célia could come back.'

'Why would you want that?'

'Because you are sad without her. And I don't want you to be sad.'

'But wouldn't you be sad, living with Meredith?'

She shrugged. 'I'd be okay.'

Loukis cursed silently. How could a ten-year-old contain such stoicism? More than he ever had even five years older when Meredith had walked out on him and his father. And that thought brought a startling revelation. He was teaching his little sister, at ten years old, exactly the same lesson that their mother had taught him.

That love had a price. Annabelle was making her own bargain with him. His happiness for hers. And that devastated him. He couldn't do it. He couldn't allow this cycle to continue. No matter the cost to himself. But in order to break that cycle, he would have to risk everything.

He opened his arms to her and Annabelle threw herself into his embrace.

'So, how was it?' Ella's voice fed into her ear from where the phone was cradled between her shoulder and head as Célia pushed the plunger down on the cafetière.

She had rejected a video call, knowing that her friend would be horrified at the way Célia looked in that moment. She sighed.

'Weird, awkward, painful, but kind of okay.'

'Well, the *kind of okay* bit is good?' she asked, rather than stated, probing for more than Célia was capable of providing.

Célia had just got back from lunch with her

parents. Both of them. Her father had aged so much in the last five years, she had been shocked. Shocked that the salt and pepper hair had transformed to a pure brilliant white. Shocked at how the lines on his face had increased in the time she had missed. Shocked that he had been so contrite, when—at the time—he had resolutely ignored any and all attempts to discuss the repurposing of her designs.

From words she'd been forced to read between, she realised that in his own way he had been hiding from the effects of his actions. A man wholeheartedly used to making quick, determined decisions about his company, he'd not quite been ready to interrogate the motives behind them.

It still hurt. That her father couldn't admit that he'd been wrong. Still awkward and distant in his feelings, he couldn't offer her the words of love and reassurance that she so desperately needed to hear. But if she wanted to be loved for who she was, she could hardly demand perfection from him. She too had to find love in imperfection, whether with her father, or herself. And that realisation had been the first step. In confronting the past she was so ashamed of. And in that bittersweet painful moment, she realised that she could no longer be bound by it. That she needed to live her life and stop hiding—as she had once accused Loukis of doing.

She poured the coffee into a mug and crossed the room of her Parisian apartment and curled up on her sofa, the phone still cradled between her shoulder and ear the way her hands now cradled the steaming cup of goodness.

'It is,' she said, finally answering Ella's half-question.

'Have you heard from him?'

Célia didn't have the energy to muster ignorance as to whom Ella was referring. 'No. But I didn't expect to,' she replied around the lump in her throat. 'Anyway, tell me about your gorgeous little one. How is Tatiana?'

'Teething.'

Célia groaned in sympathy. 'And Roman?'

'Loving everything about parenting. I'm lucky if I can get a look-in.'

'I'm sure he's just making up for the time he's away with work.'

'It's *him* I can't get a look-in with,' Ella replied quickly with a beautiful laugh. 'Tatiana only has eyes for him. For me, she has dirty nappies!'

Célia smiled, even as her heart broke. She'd have been lying to herself if she denied that she had hoped that perhaps her future could follow a similar path to her best friend's and to one day find that same happiness with Loukis.

'Are you sure you won't come down to Puy-calvel? Roman would send the jet in a heartbeat.'

'That's okay. Honestly. Yalena has returned the signed contracts and there is plenty of work to do now. It's certainly enough to keep me busy.'

'Life doesn't have to be all work, you know,' Ella chided, unconsciously cutting at Célia's heart. Because work was all she felt she had left now.

'Mmm-hmm,' she mused, noncommittally.

Célia heard a mewl in the background. One that was beginning to become insistent. 'You should go, Ella. I'll be fine. Promise.'

As she disconnected the call and placed her phone down on the table, the sapphire ring glinted in the dim light of what was quickly becoming a very late evening. She twisted the ring with her thumb, not in the least ready to remove it. It meant too much to her. The moment when she had felt finally *seen* by someone. Accepted. She threw her head back against the plush pillow resting against the arm of her sofa, growling at herself.

She had to let him go. She knew that. But she wouldn't deny the things he had brought to her. Never would she have known the feeling of empowerment resulting from being desired for who she was. Never would she have approached such an incredible client as Yalena, found a sense of pride in her work through that relationship. Never would she have reached out to her mother to ask her to arrange a lunch with her father if she had not met Loukis. If she had not realised that people made mistakes, sometimes not entirely their own fault. That love could be felt and wanted, despite events that shaped wishes into other things. Just as she loved and wanted Loukis, despite knowing her actions had brought about their separation. And though he was no longer going to be a part of her life, he had left behind those fundamental changes within her. Even as her heart ached, she felt transformed by him.

Glorious scent-laden steam wafted up from the cup of coffee. For the last three days, Célia had desperately tried to stave off sleep for as long as possible. Because at night, the dreams came. Memories mixed with fantasies, as Loukis kissed and caressed his way through the sleeping hours, leaving her to wake with tears on her eyelashes as she realised he was no longer a part of her life.

Her phone pinged with a message she would have ignored had it not been from an unknown number.

Leaning forward over the cup, she read the text.

can you call .me cherry

A spike of adrenaline sliced through her so quickly, it took her a moment to decipher the unpunctuated message.

She grabbed for the phone, immediately worried that Annabelle was in some kind of trouble, uncaring of the way she had slammed her cup on the table or the spill of dark caffeinated stain soaking into the plush white rug on the floor.

The moment the call rang through, Célia demanded to know if Annabelle was okay.

'Yes. No. Well, yes,' came the somewhat confusing reply. 'I am,' she concluded, perhaps realising how scared Célia had been in that moment.

Célia expelled a giant lungful of air and leaned back against the pillow again.

'Well, *ma chérie*, what can I do for you?' she said, somehow wrangling her voice under control, even as her pulse began a slow descent to normality.

Please don't talk about Loukis. Please.

Célia honestly didn't think she could bear it. But she was desperate to find out what happened with the court case after she had left. Had they awarded Loukis guardianship? Or had the damage been irretrievable? She drew her thumb to her mouth and bit at the nail to prevent all the questions from falling onto the shoulders of a ten-year-old girl.

'Can you come to Greece?'

'Now?'

'Yes?'

'I'm sorry, *ma chérie*, it's nearly midnight

here. There are no flights. And even then, I'm not sure—'

'It's just that the judge is deciding the custurdy thing on Wednesday. I really need you there.'

'It hasn't been—?' She cut herself off. Clearly the court case hadn't been finalised yet, but it would the day after tomorrow. 'I don't really think I should be there, Annabelle.'

'But you have to be. You *have to.*'

Célia's heart ached more than ever.

'Because Loukis will be on one bench and Mummy on the other and no one will be with me.'

Célia felt tears forming in the corners of her eyes at the mournful voice through the phone.

'Does Loukis know you're asking me?'

'No. It's a surprise!'

Not one she could imagine Loukis being happy with.

'Please don't tell him that you're coming. It will ruin it. Please, Cici. Please? Pinkie promise? I need you there. With *me.*'

As Célia made her way up the stairs of the court building she looked around furtively, hoping that she wouldn't run into anyone. The feeling was ridiculous, considering she was about to return to the courtroom itself where everyone would see her.

She hadn't had the strength to refuse Annabelle. If it had been for anyone else, she would have found it somewhere.

'*I need you there. With* me.'

It had been too much. She defied anyone to turn down the pleas of a ten-year-old girl. She pushed through the heavy swinging circular door and followed the familiar hallway towards the chamber where Annabelle's future was to be decided. Where Loukis's future would be decided too. A future that she had, albeit accidentally, put at risk.

She had already decided that if he asked her to leave, she'd go. She'd go and never come back. But Annabelle's call had lifted a lid on Célia's hopes and all the hurt and fear that came with them. She needed to know what was going to happen today.

She looked up to find Annabelle standing outside the chamber, half hanging on the large wooden door, her other arm frantically beckoning her forward as if Célia was about to miss something.

Her reluctant steps picking up speed at Annabelle's urgency, she barely had time to say hello before the little girl had grabbed her hand and led her into the courtroom. She looked up fearfully at the table where Loukis and his lawyers sat. Only the suited men she recognised from the previous court attendance turned round. Far from the way they had looked at her before—as if she were a bomb that had detonated their case—they nodded, faces grim with protocol and severity, but without censure. The judge, mid-sentence, barely acknowledged the interruption, while Meredith and her lawyers seemed glee-fully outraged. Byron, on the other hand, looked strangely miserable and deeply unhappy. Reluc-tantly her gaze was drawn to the broad outline of Loukis's shoulders, stiff and immoveable as if he were refusing even to register her attendance. He must have known, she realised, otherwise he would have turned. He would have wanted to know who had entered the court.

'I've already told them,' Annabelle said in a not-so-quiet whisper the way only a child could get away with. 'I've done my bit.'

'Your bit?' Célia asked, in a much more quiet tone. 'I thought you wanted me here for that? Am I late? You said ten-thirty?' Célia's voice gained a trace of panic as she realised that she had somehow let Annabelle down again.

'No. You're just in time.'

'Your Honour?'

Loukis's voice, rough and deep, as if he too had had many a sleepless night.

'I understand that it is time for my final statement, and, although it is an unusual one, I have a request.'

When the judge gestured for him to continue he said, 'I would like to call Célia d'Argent back to the stand to clarify some aspects of her statement.'

The whispers started between the lawyers, Meredith clearly unhappy with the new development, and Célia absolutely terrified. What on earth was Loukis doing? Was he planning to engineer a way to place *all* the blame at her feet? Was that the only way he could hope to win guardianship? If so, she could not blame him and would willingly do whatever it took to help.

Annabelle was smiling at her, pushing her forward and letting go of her hand. It was that loss that Célia felt most keenly. Unable to meet anyone's gaze, she kept her eyes on the floor as she approached the chair beside the judge. She feared that the moment she locked eyes with Loukis she might cry and that wouldn't help anyone. But when she looked up, rather than seeing hatred or vengeance in his eyes, she saw…something she couldn't hope to put a name to.

'Célia, thank you for coming today.'

She tried to keep the frown from her face, as it sounded as if he had known that she would be here. A quick glance at Annabelle's beaming face seemed to suggest that her plan was going winningly. A plan that was—contrary to her assurance—not some great surprise to Loukis.

'Five years ago, when you were working on the technical specifications for a drone tracking system, what were your hopes?'

'I'm not sure what you—'

'What was the intended use?'

Célia could give him this. She could see that he was trying to resolve the implications made the last time she was here. Felt somehow soothed by the fact that he was giving her the chance to explain. Even if it was too late.

'To help improve the tracking and data management of agricultural drones in drought-affected areas.'

'Areas such as…'

'Parts of Africa, Australia, areas in Pakistan…there are many places in the world that are drought-affected and that number is only increasing with global warming.'

'And you had no intention of that technology being used by the defence industry.'

'No. It was coursework for my degree but I had been using some of the equipment and time at my internship at Paquet.'

'And as such it was considered to come under their intellectual property disclosure.'

'Yes.'

'In fact, the use of the designs caused you great emotional stress?'

Célia bit the inside of her cheek before responding.

'Yes.'

'In what way?'

'I… It just did,' Célia replied, not quite sure what he wanted from her.

'In fact, it severely damaged your relationship with your father whom you were estranged from for nearly five years, it led you to leave a promising future in computer sciences and…it made you doubt yourself.'

His eyes bored into hers as if to say that he hated this. Hated hurting her. But she would bear it. For him.

'Yes.'

'Why did you leave me?'

The abrupt turn in questioning made Célia's stomach lurch.

'Excuse me?'

'Why did you break our engagement and leave?'

'I… Do we have to do this here?' she asked somewhat desperately.

'Yes,' he pressed resolutely. 'Why did you break our engagement?'

'Because it would risk your guardianship over Annabelle.'

'And why was that so important?'

Célia stared at him. As if she could demand to know what he was doing. Why he was putting her through this.

'Because I love you. And I've come to love Annabelle. And I don't want to see you both hurt because of my actions.'

As if the spell had been lifted, Loukis smiled, broad, wide, beautiful. His eyes sparkled and she'd never seen him look so wondrous.

'Good. Because I love you too.'

Célia's heart leapt.

'But I'll get back to that in a minute. I promise.' He turned to face the judge. 'Your Honour, if the courts are here to decide about protection, about family, then this is me. Protecting my family and fighting for the woman I love. I have a written statement from François Paquet completely freeing Célia d'Argent from any knowledge of what her technical specifications were to be used for. And I am devastated that she was so mistreated by the questions posed by my mother's lawyers, devastated that someone so good, so full of love and self-sacrifice was hurt by *my* actions and *my* needs. A woman who challenges me to be and do more each and every day, a woman who makes me a better person. And if this custody case is the price of Célia's love for me and my love for her, it is not one I'm willing to pay.

Nor am I willing to teach Annabelle that lesson either. Annabelle has told you in her own words that she would like to stay with me. Would like to maintain her life here, with her friends and family that love her. I urge you to take this into consideration in your decision. But for now, I'd very much like to kiss my fiancée if that's okay, Your Honour?'

A rueful smile played at the mouth of the wigged judge and Célia practically fled the chair, at the same time as Loukis crossed the room, and they met in the middle in a kiss that Célia would remember for the rest of her life.

She gave no heed to the chaos that erupted around them, as his lips found hers and she felt the greatest well of love spring within her. Tears once again escaped her eyes, but this time they were full of joy.

'I love you,' he whispered against her lips.

'I love you too,' she whispered back.

Finally the commotion around Meredith's lawyers' table became too intrusive, Byron's anger boiling over and Meredith's panicked voice hastily trying to call him back. The large oil baron's arm cut through the air punctuating the word 'done', and he turned, taking a few short steps towards them.

'I'm so very sorry about how painful that must have been for you,' the American said. 'It should never have happened. And while I do love her,' he said helplessly, 'I cannot condone Meredith's actions. Other than to say that desperation made her…but it is inexcusable.'

As he left the courtroom, Célia looked towards the older woman, recognising some of the devastation across her features. Because she, herself, had looked like that over the last few days and, no matter what had happened, Célia's heart ached for the woman.

Her lawyers demanded a short recess from the court, and Loukis took Célia's hand in one of his just as Annabelle launched herself towards them. They were ushered from the room and back into the small office that was suddenly bursting with frantic laughter and happy tears from Loukis, Célia and Annabelle. But all the while, concern that Loukis still might lose custody beat in her chest.

'Are you sure?' she whispered to him as Annabelle wrapped her small body around Célia's waist. 'The risk, it's too great…'

'Not as great as the risk of teaching Annabelle that love has a price. That love *is* the price. I *won't* do that.'

They gazed at each other with love blazing in their eyes. It seemed to go on for ever, Célia refusing to break the heady, half-fearful, all-joyous and all-consuming feeling bursting within her.

Until one of Loukis's lawyers knocked on the door, and entered, the smile on his face as broad as she'd ever seen.

'It's over. Meredith has dropped the case. The courts are happy to award you full guardianship. Her only request was that she be able to see Annabelle a few times a year, with your permission.'

Célia's heart soared, to see the sheer happiness and relief across Loukis's features.

She felt Annabelle tug at both of them. 'Can I, Loukis?'

'Is that something you'd like?' he asked his sister.

'Yes.'

'Then you shall.'

'Can I…go and see Mummy?'

'Of course you can,' he insisted, his eyes returning to Célia's.

The lawyer stretched his hand out to Annabelle and the two made their way out into the hallway.

Loukis looked at the woman he loved, knowing that they still had more to say. That he did.

'Can you forgive me?'

She looked so adorably confused in that moment. 'What for?' she demanded.

'For letting you go. For not realising sooner. For putting you through—'

'There's nothing to forgive, Loukis. For so

long, I was afraid of it all coming out. Of people thinking exactly what Meredith did. And I think I needed that. I needed to actually see it and feel it, to realise that it's how I see myself that matters. That I know that wasn't what I had intended. And that sometimes people do make mistakes. Unintentional ones. Like me. Like my father. How did you…?'

'I called him, told him what happened. That I loved you and asked him if he could provide a statement for the court. He was more than happy to do so and within twenty minutes of the end of our conversation, he'd emailed it through.'

'You did that for me?' she asked as if still incredulous at the lengths he would go to for her.

'I would do *anything* for you,' he replied, the promise on his lips soul-deep and eternal.

'Do you think the judge is still in the chamber?'

'No idea.' Loukis was confused as to the direction of her thoughts. 'Why?'

'Because I can't wait a minute longer to become Mrs Célia Liordis. I think it will be my most favourite name yet.'

Loukis's heart soared. This incredible woman wanted to be his wife, his future and his love. And Annabelle would be with them for every step of it. Family. The thing he'd avoided for so many years was now the only thing he wanted from the rest of his very happy ever after.

EPILOGUE

AUGUST HAD BECOME Célia's favourite month. Since their wedding—sadly not the day of the court case owing to licences and other frustrating legalities, but a beautiful day full of family, friends, flowers and the most gorgeous dress Célia had ever seen—Ella and Roman's family would come to the island for four whole magical weeks.

It hadn't been long after the wedding that Célia had discovered she was pregnant with their first child, Georgia, and then not long after their second, Antonis, much to Annabelle's great delight. With Ella and Roman's children, Tatiana, Adeline and Tikhon, Loukis would joke about opening a crèche.

But that wasn't what was occupying a large portion of Célia's recent spare time. She had gone back to university, deciding to honour her childhood dreams of computer sciences. She had no plans yet to return to the industry, but as she now well knew…plans changed and people changed with them.

Even Meredith, she ruefully acknowledged. It had taken a long time, but Loukis and his mother seemed to have found a balance and a sense of accord from their mutual love of Annabelle. The older woman had eventually apologised when she realised how much damage her actions in court had caused to others. It appeared she had truly been in love with Byron and in her desperation to be the perfect wife and mother he envisioned, she had gone too far. But Meredith had worked hard to prove her love for her fiancé as well as Annabelle and was even making tentative steps towards repairing her relationship with Loukis too.

It was the only thing that had prompted the hesitant suggestion from Loukis that perhaps the following August, they might invite Meredith for a short period. Célia had known how difficult that had been for him, but she also knew how important it was to forge those relationships—as she had done herself with her own parents. August had become the most precious time for them all. All business was put on hold and each company's workforce was given a month-long holiday to spend with their own families, because each and every one of them knew the importance of it.

As Célia checked and rechecked the fridge and pantry, ensuring that there was enough food for their first evening meal together that year, she paused—delighting in hearing the joyous sounds of Annabelle playing with Georgia and Antonis, their excitement at being reunited with Tatiana, Adeline and Tikhon. A last-minute addition of Yalena, Iannis and their family wouldn't even put a dent in all the food and produce Loukis had ordered.

'Do you think we've got enough?' her husband asked from over her shoulder.

'What, for the apocalypse? Yup. We should survive,' she replied drily.

'No one will go hungry in my house,' he declared.

'Little chance of that,' she assured him, turning towards Loukis as he reached his arms around her waist and drew her towards him. They never tired of the little touches that had brought them so close together in the early stages of their relationship. And Célia had never stopped wondering at the fact that something so wonderful, so pure, so loving could have come from such fake beginnings.

'Mmm…' she mused. 'Why is it that I'm thinking you're hungry, but not for food?' she teased.

'Because you know me so, so well.'

'I also know, *so, so well*, that our guests will be arriving in little under two hours and I've still yet to put the bedding in the spare rooms, tidy the sitting room, and clear away the playthings from the outside table.'

'Ella and Roman won't mind. They're used to it.'

'But Yalena and Iannis—'

'Will absolutely, one hundred per cent understand. Anyone who has taken one look at my beautiful wife would understand,' he assured her.

And it made her think of all the ways he'd seen her since that day in the courtroom. Flush with the excitement of their reunion, the passion he could tease from her, terrified and exhausted as her first labour went from its thirty-sixth hour into an emergency C-section, awed and infinitely full of love as she held their first child, then their second just a few years later. Grief-stricken when she had lost her father, but resolute and comforted by the way that they had found a peace between them and forged a loving relationship in those final years. But the best of it was each and every morning when she opened her eyes to find him looking at her as if he'd never seen anything more beautiful or more beloved.

The soft bent of her thoughts was yanked back to the present with an outrageous cry as he slapped her behind.

'Bedroom. Now,' he commanded with light, laughter and passion ringing his gaze.

The absolute *gall* of the gorgeous man she was proud to call her husband, the father of her children and the love of her life.

Her outrage died the moment she saw the impassioned look in his eyes and she raced him all the way to the bedroom and beyond.

* * * * *

Unable to put
Rumours Behind the Greek's Wedding *down?*
Find your next page-turner with these other stories by Pippa Roscoe!

Reclaimed by the Powerful Sheikh
Virgin Princess's Marriage Debt
Demanding His Billion-Dollar Heir
Taming the Big Bad Billionaire

Available now